The Hoodoo Princess

GHOST HUNTERS SOCIETY

Book Five

Adria Waters

Printed in the United States of America
Copyright © 2019 by Adria Waters

Published by: H2O Press

Cover by: Covered Creatively

ISBN-13: 978-1-947630-02-4

To my forever angel.
Love you, Dad.

CHAPTER 1

Lottie Adams was a young woman accustomed to getting what she wanted, and the moment she saw Jacob Smith through the lace curtains at the window of her room, she knew he would be hers. Everything about him, from the confident way he held himself, the flourish with which he carried out his sermons, the kindness he showed everyone he met, made her fall hopelessly and irreversibly in love with the man who gave sermons each week from her father's garden. Twirling a dark curl around and around her finger, she watched him from her perch above as he held revivals in the courtyard, the cords in his neck standing out as he preached the Word of the Lord.

He came every Sunday, early in the morning, the dew heavy on the grass and the Savannah air hanging hot and thick. Before he left each week, Lottie would run down and make him a glass of tea. Today, she tipped the cool liquid into a glass and as she passed the mirror in the hallway, she checked her hair. Pinching her cheeks to give them color, she ran out the kitchen door, the glass of tea sloshing as she ran to catch Jacob before he swung the wrought iron gate open to his waiting horse.

"Mr. Smith!"

He turned from tying his saddlebag, his blue eyes shaming the sky, and smiled. "How do you do, Miss Lottie?"

She cast her eyes to the ground and then looked up at him through her thick lashes, a smile turning the corners of her perfect mouth. She was a beauty and she knew it. Her father told her all the time that she was the prettiest princess in the entire world. From the time she was old enough to climb into his lap while he smoked his pipe to the day she turned eighteen, she had been the apple of her father's eye and he made sure she wanted for absolutely nothing. Given his status in the community, it was easy to do. Their family had immigrated to the United States from England when she was only a small girl and he quickly became one of the wealthiest merchants in the entire state. Their home in the southeast tything of Oglethorpe square was the most prominent in town; two stories with a massive garden, carriage house, and nearly every edifice framed by wrought iron, an outward sign of the wealth contained within.

"I thought you might like a cool drink before you go," Lottie said, offering the glass to Jacob. She stepped back as he took it from her and downed the liquid in a few loud gulps. She watched the Adams apple work in his throat.

"Much obliged, Miss." His fingers brushed hers as he handed the glass back and she almost swooned. He placed his foot in the stirrup and swung easily into the saddle of his roan. "I wish you a good afternoon." Tipping his hat, he turned his horse and headed toward River Street.

She stood there, empty glass in hand, her nerve suddenly failing her. He was almost halfway down the street when she finally got her voice to work.

"Party!" she called out.

Jacob stopped and turned to look back at her, a smile playing on his lips as his horse sidestepped.

She ran forward a few steps, her dainty shoes clicking on the brick pavers that lined the street. Panic stopped her short. *What are you doing? Father would never allow you to be this forward.* A moment later, she shook her head and tossed the thought aside. She'd never had much use for rules anyway. Drawing up, she smoothed her skirt and cleared her throat.

"Mr. Smith, my father is hosting a garden party on Friday evening in three weeks' time. My cousin, Louis, has graduated from University and we are giving him a party before he goes off to Litchfield for law school." She shook her head and took a deep breath to calm herself. "Would it please you to come?"

Jacob nudged his horse and it walked back toward her. "A garden party?"

She smiled and nodded, her curls bouncing with the motion. "Yes, so please say that you will come."

Jacob leaned over, his forearms resting on the saddle horn as he stared off in the distance. His face was so impossibly handsome and his eyes seemed even bluer as he turned them to her. "Why, yes, Miss Lottie. I believe I will be able to attend. Tell your father that I will be in attendance if he is agreeable to it."

She smiled, her heart nearly bursting from her chest. "Yes, Mr. Smith, I am sure I am most agreeable to it." Her cheeks flushed hot. "I mean, my father will be agreeable to it." She bit her bottom lip and looked at her skirt as it brushed the pavement below.

"I am glad to know the latter," he smiled when she looked up at him, "as well as the former." His horse tossed its head and then Jacob was off, his shoulders broad and strong as he rode away around the edge of the square. At the corner, he turned and raised his hand in a wave. Lottie brought her hand up in a wave to his retreating form and then ran back to her house, the smile never dropping from her face.

"I have to find something to wear," she mused, climbing the staircase to her room. Crossing to her dressing table, she sat and stared at her reflection in the mirror. The crystal teardrop lamp on the table lit her face on one side and the sunlight filtering through the Spanish moss on the huge oak tree outside her window lit the other. She regarded herself for a moment, a slow smile spreading on her face. *Beautiful.* A bead of sweat dropped delicately from her hairline to her cheek. She wiped it away and heaved herself up from the chair. It was the hottest spring she could remember and she opened the window to allow the breeze to blow through her room as she swung open the closet doors. She began pulling dress after dress from the chifforobe, considering each before tossing them on her bed.

"Oh, bother!" she pouted, flouncing onto the bed on top of all the layers of satin and lace.

Heavy boot steps on the floor announced her father and she looked up as he stood in the doorway and considered her for a moment.

"You look so like your mother at times." Otto's voice held the tinge of sadness it always did when he spoke of her mother who had died of typhoid fever before they left for the Americas. He crossed the room and passed a gentle hand along her cheek. "You have her eyes." Clearing his throat, he stood up straight. "Now, judging from your countenance. I can only imagine you have a matter of grave importance?"

Lottie gestured to the pile of dresses under her. "I have nothing to wear to the garden party!"

His mustache twitched as he took her hands in his. "My dearest, do not despair. After brunch, you must go see our dear Mr. Williams and have one commissioned."

She pouted and pulled her hands from his. "The fashions here are hideous. I want this." She picked up the fashion plates lying on her table and pointed to a dress. "This is what they're wearing in Paris. Here they are wearing, well, burlap sacks!"

"My sweet princess. Take this picture with you and have Mr. Williams work his magic. It will all be well. I promise. Now," he said, "I must return to work." He started to walk to the door.

"Father?"

He turned.

"I invited Mr. Smith, the pastor, to the garden party." She furrowed her brow and cast her eyes downward. "I am sorry if I overstepped."

Otto smiled, his frame filling the doorway of her bedroom. "Mr. Smith is, of course, welcome at our affair. Half the town will be here as it is. What is one more?"

After brunch, Lottie made her way to the northeast trust lot through the thick Savannah air, her steps quick with excitement. She climbed the few brick steps to the door of the couturier and opened the door. Once inside, the clamoring heat lessened and Lottie wandered down the dark wooden floors, pausing to inspect a hat with a peacock feather before making her way to the counter.

"Mr. Williams?" she called out, her voice lost in the ruffles of fabric surrounding her. Lottie took off her hat and placed it on the counter next to the fashion plate. "Mr. Williams," she called out again. "It's Lottie. I'm here to have a dress made."

A whisper crept from a room in the back of the store and snaked along the floor, caressing the side of the counter before oozing along the surface to

Lottie. "Here." The word sent icicles down Lottie's spine, and she shivered even as sweat pooled at the small of her back.

"Mr. Williams?" Her voice was small this time and she made her way around the counter, her footfalls silent as she craned her neck to see beyond the slightly ajar door into the room. Her fingers trembled as she pushed the door open further. A shaft of light from a large window cut into the darkness beyond, landing on a curtain of fabric drawn across the top shelves of a cabinet and shining on something behind. Lottie reached up and moved the curtain to the side. Vials, candles, and herbs lined the shelves. She leaned in close to the shelf and read the labels on some of the vials: *hotfoot oil, tooth tonic, pain relief.* A vial on the end of the shelf caught her eye. "Princess Love Potion," she whispered, taking the vial from the shelf and turning it around in her fingers.

"Your father mentioned that you might be by when we brunched today."

Lottie spun around, the vial dropping from her fingertips and shattering on the floor. "Mr. Williams! I-I heard something from this room and thought it was you."

Mr. Williams' eyes were full of concern. They dropped to the liquid spilling from the vial onto the wooden floor. The color drained from his face. "I see you, well, you have something of interest, there, child." He recovered a bit, and blinked several times. "You, no doubt, have a particular person in mind?"

Lottie's cheeks flared red and she dropped her gaze, visions of Jacob swimming in her mind's eye. Taking a breath, she gestured to the cabinet, the shelves exposed by the drawn curtain. "What are all of these?"

Mr. Williams crossed the threshold and stood staring at the bottles and vials, seeming to forget she was in the room for a moment. "Do you know how much a couturier makes in England?" He didn't wait for her answer. "Suffice it to say that it is a great deal more than a couturier in Savannah, Georgia. Harriet is accustomed to a, well, a certain way of life and I was not able to provide her that until now."

"Until now?"

He glanced at her and seemed to consider something for a moment before opening a drawer and pulling out a journal, its leather binding cracking with age. He placed it in one palm and lifted the cover slowly. As he did, something whispered out of the pages beyond. Something dark. Something sinister. And something that wound its way across the small room to Lottie, settling at her feet like an obedient mongrel.

"Contained within these pages are the ancient secrets of the root workers, the *conjurers*." Mr. Williams cocked an eyebrow, then he smiled. "Or at least, that's what the tinker who sold it to me said." He closed the journal and placed it on the shelf. Lottie's eyes never left the worn cover.

"Do they work?" she asked, moving to stand next to Mr. Williams as he gazed up at the vials, the proximity to the journal causing her skin to crawl with electricity.

He snorted. "The 'love potion' you dropped on the floor is nothing more than a mixture of orange peel, cocoa beans, orris root, and red rose petals mixed into a splash of whiskey."

Lottie sighed. "Then why do people buy them?"

"Surely you know, though, the *intent* is greater than content?" Mr. Williams grabbed a vial of pain relief off the shelf. "This tincture contains nothing more than lemon, peppermint, lavender, meadowsweet, and a healthy dose of bourbon. However," he smiled, "it does also contain the intent of the purchaser, which is the most powerful thing in the world, child. And, people pay dearly for the things that they wish to have."

"Does Father know?"

Mr. Williams shook his head. "Your father does not know of my financial burdens and, as he was the impetus behind Harriet and my journey to the Americas, it would vex him greatly to learn of our troubles."

Lottie considered journal for a moment before she tore her gaze from the leather cover. "I will never speak of this to my father." She grabbed a vial of hotfoot oil from the shelf. "This is, of course, complimentary? I would hate for Father to question a purchase on his account?"

Mr. Williams' smile faded. "Of course. Now, you have need of a dress?" He walked to the doorway and waited.

"Yes, sir. For the garden party in honor of my cousin." Fingers of icy hot insistency reached out from the journal, clutching at her arm. Her breath caught in her throat.

"Then, it shall be one of the most beautiful dresses for one of the most beautiful young ladies in all of Savannah."

As he turned his back, Lottie's hand darted out and she grabbed the journal. She stuffed it into her reticule. Her heart raced and her insides hummed.

"*The* most beautiful young lady," she said, a smile twisting her features.

Mr. Williams glanced back at her, worry knitting his brow. "Y-yes, of course."

***

Three weeks later, Lottie stood sentry at the gate, watching the street for Jacob as she smoothed the skirt of the beautiful pink dress she had commissioned. She rubbed a dainty lace gloved hand along the top of the wrought iron, her nerves on edge as she reached up to pinch her cheeks. Her waist had been drawn in by her corset, creating miniscule proportions which only allowed her to take small breaths of hot air. Late spring had already set its teeth into Savannah and the breezes were few and far between. Lottie bit her bottom lip, ignoring the sounds of the party going on behind her in the garden.

Her foot touched on the loose dirt near the base of the oak tree where the furry recipients of her still developing talents lay. While Mr. Williams' interpretation of the knowledge contained within the pilfered journal was limited to what he thought profitable, Lottie devoured every word with purpose, her unrequited love for Jacob moving her to dark places only hinted at by the words on the page. Her first success had come just a week ago when the housecat had merely vomited and then stared out from under the bed with petulant green eyes. He was sick for hours, but he lived. After that, Lottie had met with other successes which galvanized her to attempt her plan today. One that would make him fall in love.

A carriage turned the corner and parked in front of their house. Lottie leaned out to look around the magnolia bushes flanking the gate, hoping to see Jacob emerge, but alas, it was only her uncle, followed by Louis, the guest of honor. She turned to tell her father of their arrival when she saw her uncle holding his hand out for someone else climbing from the carriage. Rolling her eyes, she stared as Louis' sister emerged, a buttery yellow skirt spilling out around her. Even in last season's style, she was the picture of grace and beauty and Lottie felt the pinpricks of jealousy run along her spine. If Lottie was the prettiest young woman in Savannah, her cousin was a close second. At that moment, the sound of hoof beats from the opposite end of the street reached her ears and she whirled around to see Jacob riding up. He looked as handsome as ever, and as the afternoon's colors wound their way around the square, they seemed to make him even more captivating.

With a rush of adrenaline, Lottie pulled the vial from her glove and pulled the stopper. Closing her eyes, she repeated the words she had learned and summoned all of her strength before dropping the sluggish red liquid into her mouth. Bile rose as she swallowed, the liquid coating her throat. Waiting a beat for any immediate ill effects, she rushed out to greet him as he got down from his horse and passed the reins to the stable hand. Her uncle and cousins reached him first, her uncle pumping Jacob's hand up and down in greeting. Lottie stood near, her stomach flipflopping, threatening to empty its contents on the ground in front of her as she manifested the smoky tendrils and sent them out toward Jacob. They danced along the ground, skipping sinisterly toward his boots as he greeted Louis and then turned to raise her cousin's hand in greeting. He paused to look deep into her cousin's eyes as he bent to kiss her hand. The smoke tendrils evaporated with a snap and Lottie let out a sigh of exasperation and pushed her way forward.

"We are delighted you were able to attend," Lottie said, dipping low into a curtsy. "Come, the garden is this way."

Jacob took his hat off and bowed to her, a smile lighting his features as he stood and offered his arm. She took it, the warmth from his body radiating into her skin as she led him along the winding brick path to the garden.

The rest of the evening passed in a blur. He couldn't take his eyes off her, and in dance after dance, he spun her around as if she were a tiny ballet dancer. Love radiated from them, so it wasn't a surprise to anyone when Jacob asked for her hand in marriage after a short courtship. The Adams' garden was to be the location of the biggest wedding during the summer of 1806 and all of Savannah's most prominent members would be in attendance. Lottie watched as the plans sprung up around her. The house and garden were decorated, the menus were created, and the entire town was talking about the upcoming wedding. She walked through the house in a fog, her faculties in complete overload as the preparations were made.

One day, her father caught her hand as she walked by him in the sitting room. His eyes were full of concern as he regarded her. "Sit," he said quietly.

Lottie drew up a footstool and sat gingerly on its edge. She peered up at him.

"My dearest daughter, what has you so concerned?"

She cleared her throat, the thought that had been rattling around in her head for weeks finally becoming clear. Taking a deep breath, she blurted out her troubled thoughts. "Father, Jacob wants to be married, but he also wants to pursue his passion of spreading the Word of the Lord." She rushed on, afraid that if she stopped, even if for a moment, she would lose her nerve. "I-I do not wish for him to go, but I know in his heart that he wants to reach more people than just those of Savannah. We spoke about this and he wants to ride a circuit."

Otto regarded her again and then lit his pipe. "A circuit rider leads a very dangerous, very difficult life."

"I-I know!" She felt dangerously close to crying, but she bit back her tears. "I do not know why he wants to pursue this, but I believe that he thinks it will allow him to move up in the Methodist church."

Her father sat back, crossing his legs with the motion, a circle of smoke rising above him. Lottie could almost see the wheels turning in his head. The fact that Jacob wanted to move up his position in society would appeal to her father's sensibilities about Jacob's ability to provide for his new bride.

"I thought, perhaps," she said gently, "you could speak to the clergy to have him sent to a safe place?"

Otto nodded and then sat up. "If this is his decision, then I will do all in my power to have him sent to the safest place we can find. I know there are some new settlements in Missouri, with the Ioway more scattered and not as cohesive as the Cherokee and Creek in our area." He grew pensive as he leveled his gaze at her and took her hand. "My brave daughter, always seeing the providence in people and showing kindness and thoughtfulness. You, my dear, are of the most generous soul. I will send for Bishop Andrew and we will put this in motion for Jacob. Is this the matter that has been vexing you these past weeks?"

Lottie nodded, bile rising in the back of her throat as she thought of the two long years without her love that faced her upon his departure to the wilds of Missouri. Tears filled her eyes.

Otto drew her to him, his voice rumbling in his chest as he spoke. "My dearest, I detest seeing you in this state. My sweet, sweet soul." A moment later, he held her at arm's length, his fingers gripping her upper arms. "A gift."

Lottie shook her head. "A gift?"

"A gift for the groom. Something with which to remember what he is leaving behind in Savannah so that he might come back sooner."

A smile grew on Lottie's face and the churning in her stomach lessened a bit. "A gift. What shall I get him?"

Otto stood up and walked across the room to the grand fireplace. He motioned to the massive painting hung over the marble mantle. A woman with locks of long dark hair cascading over her shoulder sat on a chair in the garden. A smile played upon her rose lips and her cheeks were the color of her silken dress.

"I-I do not understand. He will not be able to take a painting with him on horseback."

Otto turned to look at Lottie, a chuckle bubbling up. "No, my dear. Have a painting commissioned and place it in something he can take with him."

Her brow creased.

He crossed and took her hands in his, his eyes peering into hers. "A locket."

She stared at the painting a moment longer, a dark smile parting her lips.

Yes, a locket. It's perfect.

CHAPTER 2

"So, who's up for a road trip?"

Silence met Andy's question. It stretched on in the living room for one minute, two, and then everyone started talking at once.

"Savannah?"

"What are we supposed to do when we get there?"

"We're going to travel halfway across the country on the advice of a locket?"

Andy sat next to me and patted my leg. *They'll get to it.*

What?

The fact that, in order to lift this curse, we have to go to Savannah.

I shook my head. "I don't understand. The curse is here in Culvers Grove. What good would going to Savannah do?"

All eyes turned to me, then to Andy.

"What did you hear when you held the locket?" Tristan asked quietly, his eyes searching Andy's.

"Just the one word over and over again: Savannah."

"Do you think that's where, um, Martin was from?" Evie asked.

Just then, Grandma came into the living room and stood, rubbing her upper arm with a dry, raspy hand.

I jumped up and crossed to her. "How's Grandpa?"

"The trip here was hard on him, but it's better that he's home." Her eyes were worried. "I need to get back in the kitchen, but I wanted to check on you young folks."

"We're all doing all right." I swallowed. "Dad, well, he's still not himself."

She nodded. "I checked in on him a bit ago. He's resting quietly." Grandma took a deep breath and then fixed me with a steady gaze. "He will get better, Marissa. It will simply take a bit of time. He will get better. You understand me?"

I blinked back tears and nodded.

Evie cut me off. "Savannah it is. Let's get packed." She put her arm around my shoulders and guided my back through the front door.

"See?" Andy said as he came in and shut the door behind him. "I told you all we were going on a road trip. Savannah or bust, right?"

I pressed my lips together. "We still don't know what we're doing."

He smiled and pulled me to him roughly in a one-armed hug. "Never do, Anderson. Never do."

CHAPTER 3

"Almost ready, St. Louis?" Evie stood in the doorway of my room, a duffel bag slung over her shoulder. I'd packed in record time, but now all of my energy was gone. I slumped on the bed and rubbed my forehead. The locket strained against the material of my T-shirt where I tucked it.

Evie came over to sit next to me. "You all right?" She bumped me with her shoulder.

I shook my head. "What are we going to do with Dad? He can't stay here alone."

"He's got your grandma and grandpa."

I shook my head again. "He might as well be here alone. Grandpa's not himself and neither is Grandma, for that matter. He can't see them anyway."

"Can he come with us?" Evie asked in a small voice.

I looked up at her. My throat felt strangled as the words came through. "He's not strong enough to make the trip."

"What about Melanie?" Grant asked from the doorway. "She's the only one who knows about what's going on in this town."

"He's right," Evie said. "What do you think?"

I considered it and when I couldn't come up with a good reason not to ask her, I picked up my phone. My stomach flip-flopped while I waited for her to answer.

"Hello?"

"Hi, Mrs. Ingalls. This is Marissa, Johnny's daughter."

"I know who you are! You brought my Tommy back to me!" Her voice dropped then. "You know, it was the strangest thing. I haven't been able to see him all day. I know he's still here, a mother knows these things, but I can't seem to make him out anymore. Maybe I need new glasses?"

I swallowed hard. "Um, Mrs. Ingalls, we were wondering if you would do us a big favor. We have to leave for a short trip and Dad can't come with us and we were wondering..."

She chuckled. "Bring him on over. The more the merrier. It'll be nice to have some company. I'll have to air the mattress in the spare bedroom and go grocery shopping, since I think all I have here is hamburger. He still likes pork chops, doesn't he?"

I nodded my head, but then realized that she couldn't see the motion. Sweeping my hand across my eyes, I said, "Yes, he does, but listen, I need to tell you something. Dad's not, um, well, he's not really himself right now. He's a little mixed up and I'm not sure how long it's going to last or if he's even going to come out of it." My voice caught in my throat and I looked up at Grant helplessly.

He crossed over to me, gently taking the phone from my hands. "Yes, Mrs. Ingalls, I understand. We will. Yes. We'll bring him over soon. Thank you. I will." He handed my phone back to me and placed his hand on my shoulder. "She says to bring him over as soon as we can. Don't worry; she'll take care of him."

I shook myself out from under his touch. "I don't want to leave him. This doesn't feel right." I stood up and immediately fell back to the bed. My legs weren't working.

"They're pulling on your energy, aren't they?" Evie asked, looking toward the bank of windows.

I nodded. "Yeah."

"We have to get you out of town." Grant put his arms around me and pulled me to my feet. "Let's go."

Evie led the way to Dad's bedroom across the hall and knocked softly. She turned the knob and stuck her head inside. "Mr. A? Can I come in?"

His voice sounded garbled with sleep. "Genevieve?"

My heart leapt. "Dad!" I ran to his door. "Dad?"

He sat up in bed and reached over to turn on the lamp. "Genevieve? What's wrong?"

I went in and sat on the bed next to him. "Hey, Dad. We have to take you over to Melanie's house for a little while."

He stared at me vacantly for a moment, and then something crossed his eyes. "Is your mom all right? I thought I heard her calling."

I bit back tears. "Mom's all right. You have to get up and get dressed, Dad, okay?"

He threw back the covers and crossed to his bathroom, stopping to take the pile of clothes Evie handed him. I made up his bed, tears clouding my vision, and then sat hard, the rush of adrenaline passing.

"Come on," Grant said, offering his hand. "Let's get you out of here."

I looked over at Evie.

"I've got him, St. Louis. You go on ahead."

I left her standing at his bathroom door and allowed Grant to help me navigate the hallway and the stairs. When we got to the kitchen, he pulled a chair out for me and I sat.

"He doesn't even know me," I whimpered.

Grant bent to peer into my eyes. "He will. In time, he will."

I wished I felt as confident.

"I'm going to check on Andy and Tristan. See what else needs to be done before we leave."

I nodded and rested my head in my hands on the table. Grandpa sat next to me, rocking back and forth in his chair. The wrinkles on his face deepened as he stared blankly at me. I hated that look and turned my chair away from him.

"He's right, you know." Grandma came in from the dining room, drying her hands on her apron.

"About what?" I mumbled.

"They'll all come back to us, Marissa. Give it some time."

Andy came into the kitchen as Evie led my dad down the stairs. Tristan and Grant followed.

"Everything's ready, Anderson. I'm going to take you to the outskirts of town while Tristan, Grant, and Evie take your dad to Melanie's."

I shook my head. "I want to go."

"You're a liability."

"Ouch." I narrowed my eyes at Andy.

"What he means," Tristan said pointedly, "is that you have the locket and it's becoming too dangerous to keep it in town."

"Yeah, what he said. We locked everything up and turned down the heat."

Tristan nodded. "School's out until Tuesday, so we have about five days to get there and back."

"What did you tell our parents?" Andy asked as he threw the strap of my bag over his shoulder.

Tristan waggled his eyebrows. "I told them that we were headed to visit Stanford. Dad was over the moon."

I looked at Grant. "What about yours?"

"My parents assumed I was headed back to KC already."

"Where are we going to stay when we get to Savannah?" I asked.

Everyone stared blankly at me.

"And, how are we going to afford gas, food, incidentals?"

"I have a little money in my account," Grant said, "but I won't be flush again until I get my scholarship money in a few weeks."

"I have my parent's credit card, but I won't be able to explain charges in the east when we're supposed to be headed west."

I never seemed to have any money, so I was no help.

"Hold on!" Evie handed her bag to Andy and darted out through the dining room. She was back in a few seconds, holding up an envelope. "The check from the church!"

"You can't use that," I said. "You were going to use it for college, remember?"

She shrugged. "This is more important right now. I'll get it cashed at the first bank we come to in the morning." She tucked it into her messenger bag and smiled. "See? I helped."

"Thanks, kid," Andy said, rubbing a fist across the top of her head.

She swiped at him. "Knock it off!"

The normalness of the interaction filled me with warmth and I smiled at my friends. "Thanks, guys." I pushed myself up from the table and almost fell back into the chair.

"It's getting bad, isn't it?" Evie asked.

I nodded weakly.

"Let's get you out to my truck." Andy put his arm around me and lifted me to my feet. They weren't responding and I felt bad hanging from him like a limp, wet towel.

Grandma stepped forward. "Tell him to hold on a minute."

Hold on, Andy.

Grandma looked into my eyes and reached out to take my hand. My palm tingled and I looked down to see energy arcing from her hand into mine and working its way up my arm.

"Grandma, no! You can't spare your energy." I tried to pull my hand away, but she held onto it tightly.

"I'll be the judge of what I can and can't do, thank you very much." She furrowed her brow as she sent her energy into me.

In a few moments, I was able to stand on my own and felt rejuvenated, as if I'd had a six-pack of soda and some chocolate-covered espresso beans.

Grandma took her hand away and cradled it against her chest. "It won't last long, but it'll get you to the edge of town."

I nodded. "Thank you, Grandma. I love you."

She smiled and patted my arm with her other hand. "Good luck, Marissa," her eyes welled up, "and come back to us soon."

I nodded again and followed the group out to the back porch, locking up the back door while Grant and

Evie shuffled my dad into the back seat of Grant's car. I made my way to Andy's truck. Grant trotted over and opened the door for me after he turned on his car and started the heat.

"Take care of yourself and we'll see you soon," he said, leaning in to fasten my belt. His lips brushed my cheek and then he was gone, jumping into his car and slamming the door. His headlights swung across the barn as he turned. Andy's truck roared to life and he backed up, his hand brushing my shoulder as he looked over the back seat.

"You ready for this, Anderson?"

I clasped the locket in my hand. "Yeah, I guess I have to be, right?"

He glanced at me as he turned to drive forward. "Spoken like a true hero." He chuckled as he switched the gearshift into drive.

I took a deep breath and watched Grant's tail lights disappear around the corner of the house. We followed and as the front yard came into view, I sat up and cried out.

"What's wrong?"

"They're swarming his car!" I yelled.

Dozens of ghosts were descending upon the car, their hands grasping at the windows and door handles as Grant's car slid through the mass.

"They're fine, Anderson. It's you they're after."

"Gee, thanks."

Grant's car made it through without incident and then it was our turn. I reached over to push the lock down on my door and slumped back into the seat. As Andy's truck moved into the center of the group, visions began slamming into my consciousness. They moved so rapidly from one to the other that I couldn't hold onto any of them for more than a moment.

...Help me! Please! I'm in so much pain!...

...so lonely. Where's my little girl? I miss her...

...it burns! Make the flames go away! Please...

...Please...

...Help me!

I turned to Andy as a strangled cry escaped my lips.

"Hold on, Anderson!"

I felt the truck accelerate, and then everything went black.

CHAPTER 4

"Anderson?"

My eyelids fluttered.

Are we outside the barrier? I forced my eyes open and peered out. "It's dark," I said, my mouth full of cotton.

"Thanks, Señorita Obvious."

"I can't see in the dark," I slurred, trying to shake the vestiges of sleep from my mind. "Turn on the lights."

Andy turned the signal bar and the headlights flipped on, flooding the land in front of us with bright white light.

My hand flew to my mouth as I sat up. "Yeah, um, we're outside the barrier." I watched as about fifty spirits pressed against the invisible wall, the mass undulating as they tried to reach out. I described it to Andy. "It reminds me of all the spirits pressing against the smoke in the cavern beneath the courthouse," I said quietly.

Andy turned the headlights off, plunging us into darkness again, the only lights remaining from the digital clock which blinked 6:32 and a muted purple glow from inside my shirt. I zipped my coat up to my chin, drowning out the light. The frigid night lay in wait outside, but we were warm in our little cocoon in the cab of the pickup truck. We sat in silence for a few minutes.

I cleared my throat. "Can I ask you a question?"

"You just did."

"What did you see down there? I mean, when you went into the smoke?"

My eyes slowly adjusted to the darkness and I watched the muscle in his jaw work as he stared out the windshield. He was quiet for so long that I was afraid I had offended him and I opened my mouth to apologize but clamped it closed as he started to speak.

"At first, I didn't see anything." His voice was soft, so unlike his usual brash tone, and he continued to stare straight ahead as he spoke. "The pain was awful. It, um, it felt like I was being turned inside out. I was cold and hot all at the same time and then everything hurt at once. I broke my arm when I was ten and it felt like that, except all over my body." He stopped for a moment, running his hand absently along his arm. "I saw a light through the blackness so I made my way toward it. The smoke grabbed at my feet and held me back, but I fought my way to the light. It was like I knew that the pain would stop if I made it out there, you know?" He glanced over at me.

I nodded my head.

"Anyway, when I got to the light, the physical pain stopped." He swallowed.

"What happened?"

Andy took a deep breath. "Remember how you said that you thought it showed you the thing you were most afraid of?"

I nodded again. "Yeah. For Evie, it was my dad and me ignoring her and then blowing up. And for Sam, it was his daughter burning alive." I shuddered and wrapped my coat more closely around me.

"Tristan left me. When I got to the light, he was walking away. I called out to him but he left anyway. He left and he didn't even turn back." His voice hitched a bit. "I was alone, Anderson. He was gone." Andy sat quietly for a moment. Then, he turned to me. "And, you know what the biggest bite of all is?" He shrugged. "It's happening."

"What do you mean?"

"He's leaving for school after this year. We have a few months together and then he's leaving for Stanford. He'll be gone." Andy's chin trembled. "I don't know what I'm going to do without him."

"Have you talked to him about it? Told him how you feel?"

Andy shook his head. "Not really. He changes the subject every time I bring it up."

"Well, then you have to keep trying. Show him you're willing to fight for him, for your relationship."

Andy ran the back of his hand across his nose. "Everything's going to change."

"Change isn't always bad."

He glanced over at me. "Personal experience?"

"Listen, I thought my life was over when my mom died. It hurt all the time. I didn't get to see her anymore. Ever. And, then we had to sell the house in St. Louis and move all the way out to a tiny little town in the middle of nowhere. I was in a place where I had no friends and I was lonelier than I've ever been."

"Does this have a point?" He sniffed and wrapped his arms around his middle.

I smiled. "Yes. If things hadn't changed, I would never have met you guys, or realized that my dad is one of the strongest people I know or that Culvers Grove feels more like home than St. Louis ever did. Change means things are different. Not good different or bad different, just different."

"But, your mom's still gone." His voice was quiet.

I swallowed hard. "Yes, she is, but without change, I would still be in that big house, wandering around living in the pain of losing her. Now, I get to choose what parts, what memories I get to take with me."

He was quiet for a long time. "That's beautiful, Anderson." He snickered.

"Shut up." I pushed his shoulder good-naturedly. "Promise me you'll talk to him about it?"

"I promise. Now, can we talk about something less depressing?"

I leaned my head back against the seat. "How long was I out?"

"Not that long, really. Not like usual anyway. I had just made it here and turned the truck around when you started waking up."

"Thanks, Grandma," I mumbled. The locket pushed against my coat and then thumped back heavily on my chest.

Andy looked at me. "It's outside the barrier now. Is it burning you?"

I shook my head. "No, but it's pulling harder now. Like it would fly to Savannah itself if I'd take it off the chain."

"It's not pointing to the east, though." He pointed behind him. "It's pulling back toward town."

I looked down and unzipped my coat a bit. "Look," I breathed.

The locket glowed through my shirt, emitting a deep green glow.

"Wasn't it purple before?" Andy asked.

"Yeah. I don't know what's happening."

"Maybe Jacob is overpowering Martin, you know, trying to get to all those spirits pressing up against the barrier."

Andy's words sent a shiver from my neck to my toes. I pulled the locket from my shirt and stared at it. The locket bathed my palm in its sinister green glow. "We need to leave. Soon."

"Let me see it." He reached out to touch the locket.

Be careful.

I got this, Anderson.

He drew in a breath through his teeth as his fingertips made contact. "It's hot."

"I don't feel it." I knit my brows. "Maybe it's warm because I had it next to me inside my coat?"

He shook his head and concentrated on the locket, his fingertip flat on its surface. His brow furrowed.

"What do you see?"

"It's different than before. It's as if I'm seeing two different points of view. Like, there's someone new here."

"Martin's in there, now, right?"

He nodded. "Right. I see you standing with Martin in the cavern. He's, well, you're right; she's a girl now. Weird. A guy is stepping out of the cloud and he's coming toward you, fast. He's so angry! Here comes Martin, though. She's holding out her hand. He says the name Charlotte, then, he reaches out for Martin's hand – he says it's his daughter? She has the locket hidden behind her back and now they are both being pulled into the locket." He drew his hand back and shook it. "Whoa."

"Yeah, I know." I cleared my throat. "Do you remember the vision we saw of Jacob in the locket?"

Andy stuck his fingertip in his mouth. "Yeah," he said around it before taking it out and blowing on it.

"He was reading a letter from his dearest Charlotte. She said his daughter missed him even though she hadn't met him yet?"

"Yeah, I don't remember her name, though. The baby's."

I shook my head. "Me neither, but what if Martin was somehow his daughter?"

"Maybe." He blew on his finger again. "My finger hurts."

I sat up. "Someone's coming."

The headlights grew larger as the car approached. Andy flashed his and they slowed as they came nearer. Grant's car pulled up alongside and Andy rolled his window down.

"Everything go okay?"

Grant nodded. "Yeah. We dropped him off with Mrs. Ingalls and she said she'd take care of him and call us if anything happens. You guys ready?"

"Yeah, let me get turned around and I'll follow you into Chillicothe. We'll leave the truck there in the Wal-Mart parking lot. No one will notice it there for a few days."

"See you there," Grant said and winked at me before rolling his window up and heading out along the snowy ruts in the gravel road.

Andy turned the truck and followed.

"So, if Martin was his *daughter*, why was her ghost male?" I asked, tucking the locket beneath my shirt again.

He glanced over at me then back at the road. "I don't know."

I waited a few minutes, my mind turning things over. "And, where's Charlotte? If both Jacob and Martin were in Culvers Grove, then is Charlotte in

Savannah? Or is she in the locket? Was she the one pulling everyone in?"

"I don't know."

"Could you see into Martin's past now that she's in the locket? Like, will it give you both the memories we've seen before, and the new ones? Would we be able to find Charlotte by looking at Martin's memories?"

"Anderson?"

"Yeah."

"Can we just assume my answer to every question you ask from here on out will be 'I don't know'?"

CHAPTER 5

"We're a little over five hours from Capiza, Kentucky," Tristan said from the back seat. "Can you drive that long or do you want me to look for something closer?"

"Could you look for something we've actually heard of? What about Nashville?" Grant asked.

"That's Tennessee, and another hour and a half away. Besides, I found a motel we can afford in Capiza."

We had pooled all of our money together in the parking lot in Chillicothe and come up with enough for a tank of gas, a cheap meal or two, and a modest motel room, but little else.

"I can do five hours," Grant said, looking over his shoulder at Tristan. "If I get tired, we'll stop before that."

We passed through Hannibal, Missouri and were headed south on the long, dark stretch of Highway 61, surrounded by farmland. The car was warm and quiet; the only sound was the tires humming on the highway. My stomach turned over and I tried to concentrate on the horizon, but the sun had set hours before and I could only see the gray pavement illuminated by the headlights. I burped and held the back of my hand over my mouth.

"We'll be in Troy in about an hour," I said. "It's where my mom was from."

After Troy, it would be another hour until we hit St. Louis. I settled into the passenger seat and glanced down at the locket. Since leaving Culvers Grove, it had returned to the purple color and seemed content to lie against my chest. I told the group about Andy reading it earlier and about what he saw. Grant suggested we have Andy try it again when we got to the motel, and out of a moving vehicle.

I turned my head, resting my forehead against the cool window. The steady hum of the tires lulled me and I dozed off. A few minutes later, a bump in the road jolted me and I woke with a start.

"Sorry," Grant mumbled.

I looked over at him. He was bent over, holding his stomach, and his face was pale.

"Grant? What's wrong?"

He grimaced and I looked down. Blood oozed out from between his fingers, dark red and viscous as it dripped from his fingers onto his jeans. The car swerved.

"Grant!" I yelled. "Help him!" I turned to the group in the backseat.

Andy was wrapped in black smoke and it poured from his empty eye sockets. His body twitched and jerked and the smoke burned his skin where it touched. Tristan lay still, his head back on the headrest, part of his face dripping off his skull and Evie's hair had turned to spiders, their legs waving in the air as she screamed.

Let me in, Marissssa.

A bump in the road jolted me and I woke with a start, my heart racing.

"Sorry," Grant mumbled.

I looked him over. No blood. Then, I whipped around to look at the back seat. Everyone was fine. Bored and quiet, but fine. I turned again and looked at the locket. The purple color was now mixed with the green, the muddy mixture making me nauseated. Words and images crept into my consciousness: *snot, vomit, dead things.*

"Can you pull over for a minute?" I choked down a belch as my stomach roiled.

Grant glanced over at me and flipped on his blinker. He pulled over on the shoulder and I shoved the door open before the car had completely stopped. I rolled out, holding my stomach as I put some space between the car and me. I stood in ankle-deep snow and retched several times.

"Anderson gets carsick?"

"Only on long trips," I yelled over my shoulder.

"Oh, this is gonna be delightful."

I flipped him off and leaned over my knees, my head hanging as I let the cold air clear the fog in my brain. Snow crunched behind me.

"Get back in the car," I said. "You don't want to see this."

Grant shoved his hands into his pockets. "It's fine. My mom used to have the same problem. We'll stop at the next gas station and get you some crackers and clear soda, and some motion sickness medicine." Grant put his arm around my shoulders. "Are you going to make it a few more minutes? We're only about ten minutes away from civilization."

I nodded and wiped my mouth with the back of my hand. "Gum?"

He smiled. "Yeah, in the car."

I took the arm he offered and let him walk me back to the car. I settled into the passenger seat and he waited for a semi to pass before he got back in and buckled up.

"Here," he said, passing me a container of gum.

I took it gratefully and looked down at the locket. It remained a muddy color, but more purple mud than green at this point. The nausea faded and I managed a half-hearted smile as Grant turned the car back onto the highway.

We stopped at a gas station in Troy for supplies, bathroom breaks, and a top off on the gas tank. I went inside and followed the signs to the restroom in the back. A bucket of dirty mop water sat in the hallway and I skirted around it, trying not to look at the small bits of dirt and hair floating on the top.

In the restroom, I closed the door and leaned my back on it, grateful for the coolness of the metal. Breathing deeply, I pushed away from the door and slid the latch over to lock it. The water in the sink took a while to get warm and I grabbed a paper towel while I waited. My eyes flitted up to the mirror over the sink. *Big mistake.* My reflection reminded me of when we were in the hotel in Chillicothe. My glassy eyes had huge dark circles under them and my hair hung limply around my face. I drew my mouth into a thin line and raked a brush through my hair, then pulled it up into a high ponytail.

"That's a little better," I whispered to my reflection. I didn't know what to do about the circles under my eyes, but decided that in the dark car, no one would notice anyway. As I looked, though, I saw something along my neckline. I leaned in closer to the mirror, tracing the red line from the back of my neck to the other side with a shaking finger. The constant movement of the locket was rubbing the chain along my neck, chaffing it. "Lovely," I said, turning from the mirror and zipping up my coat. I opened the door and almost ran into Grant.

He smiled and grabbed my shoulders to stop my forward momentum. "Hey, there!"

"Um, hey." My eyes darted to the rest of the store to take stock of all of my friends' locations. Andy and Tristan stood by the wall of sodas, arguing over which bottled water was the best while Evie trolled the candy aisle.

"Are you sure you're all right?" Grant asked.

I swung my gaze back to him. "Yeah, um, why?"

He didn't let go of my arms as he peered into my eyes. "Because you look terrible."

"Seriously?"

He chuckled softly. It was a comforting sound and I dropped my guard.

"You look like you've been through a lot in the past few days," he said, "and I want to make sure you're up for this."

"This trip?" I ticked my eyebrow up.

"This trip and what you'll have to do when we get to Savannah."

I swallowed. "I don't even know what that will be."

"But you're afraid it's going to be bad."

"Aren't you?"

He took a deep breath. "Terrified."

I nodded. "Yeah, so am I."

"I'll be there the whole time, though. You know that, right?"

"I know. That's what I'm afraid of. What if you get hurt again?"

"I'll be fine," he said, enveloping me in a hug. "Ow!" he pushed away from me.

"What's wrong?"

"I-I don't know. Something burned me." He looked down at my chest and then pulled the fob on my jacket zipper. I put my hand up to stop him but he gently pushed it away. As soon as the zipper was opened a few inches, the locket glowed, muddy colors swirling along its surface.

I looked up apologetically at Grant's face.

He furrowed his brow. "Is it hurting you?"

His voice held such concern I almost teared up.

"No, it's not. Not really. I don't feel it burning like you or Andy do."

"Look at your neck!" He reached out to caress my neck then drew his hand back. "You can't wear it anymore. We have to figure out a way to keep you safe."

Andy and Tristan joined us and then motioned Evie over.

"What's going on?" she asked.

"Look at her neck," Grant gestured.

"I'm fine," I said, attempting to zip my coat back up. "Come on, the cashier's looked back here, like, four times already."

"Could we wrap it in a coat and put it in the trunk?" Tristan offered, though he didn't seem very keen on the idea of having it unattended so close to him in the backseat.

"We have to try something. She's in pain."

"I'm fine," I repeated, but I didn't feel fine. Having that thing hanging from my neck felt like the weight of the world balanced on the thin chain.

"I'll put the stuff on my card," Grant said. "You guys get her outside and get that thing off her. Here." He tossed his keys to Andy.

Andy nodded and led our little group outside. He opened the trunk and we huddled near its yawning maw.

"Take it off, St. Louis, and put it in my coat again, like you did to take it to your great-grandma's house." Evie held her coat out and looked up at me with unwavering eyes.

I licked my lips. Reaching up, I pulled the chain from around my neck and then carefully up over my ponytail. I let the chain go and opened my hand to catch the locket. Except, the locket didn't fall into my palm as I had expected it would.

"Oh, man," Andy breathed. "That's not good."

My heart skipped a beat and I looked down to see what he was staring at. The locket was firmly attached to my chest, lodged deep within the V shape of my neckline. I reached up to grasp it and gave it a tug.

Nothing. Panic welled and I looked up at my friends. "It's stuck. *On* me!"

"Well, pull it off," Andy provided.

"I'm trying," I said, gripping the golden edges with my fingernails. I yanked again and cried out. "It hurts."

"What's going on?" Grant walked up to the back of his car.

I turned to him. "It's stuck on me."

"It's *what*?" He leaned in and tried to grab it, but quickly yanked his hand back as if he'd been bitten. "I don't understand."

Tears welled up in my eyes as I looked at him. "Me neither."

"We were outside the barrier when you took it from me, right?" Grant looked around at the group. "Weren't we?"

Evie nodded. "She took it from your hands and placed it in the coat."

"Then why is it doing this now?" he asked. When no one answered, he said again, louder, "Why?"

"It's okay, Grant," I said, trying keep the tremor from my voice. "It doesn't hurt."

"Jacob wasn't in there last time. Now he's trying to get inside you like the smoke did."

I turned to stare at Evie.

She stepped closer. "Remember how the smoke tried to get inside you? The smoke was an extension of Jacob. Now that he's in the locket, maybe he's still trying to do it." She stared at me with her electric-green eyes. "And, I suspect that if Martin wasn't in there pushing back, he'd already have done it."

The gravity of her statement shook me. I quelled the panic from rising again and took a deep breath. "What do I do?"

"As long as Martin is in there, he'll keep you safe, right?" She looked around the group for confirmation. "Right?"

"Sure. Sure, that sounds right," Andy said. He raised his eyebrows.

I nodded. "It's all we have. So, let's get to Savannah so we can stop Jacob and Charlotte."

Grant didn't look convinced.

Evie reached over and patted him on the shoulder. "It will be fine. She's strong."

"Let's just hope strong *enough*," Andy muttered as he folded himself into the backseat again.

CHAPTER 6

Hours later, we pulled into the town of Capiza, Kentucky. Grant nosed the car onto the deserted Main Street and stopped at the lone light swinging in the early morning night.

"Where's the hotel?" he asked over his shoulder.

Evie nudged Tristan and he awoke with a start.

"Um, next right after the gas station." His voice was scratchy as he sat up and stretched.

Grant went forward as the light turned green.

"Reminds me of Culvers Grove after ten p.m.," Evie commented.

"Think anything's open?" Andy's voice was accompanied by an audible stomach growl.

"Did you plan that?" Evie teased.

The car went around the closed gas station and we caught our first look at the motel Tristan had scouted for us.

"Looks perfect," Grant mused. "Like the start of a horror movie. Didn't the website have pictures?"

"You try to find something better with our limited resources, man," Tristan said. "I did the best I could. It's got four-star ratings from everyone who's stayed here and it's not on the bed bug registry."

Andy snickered. "There's a *bed bug registry*?"

"Hey, there's a diner up there." Evie pointed from the backseat. "Looks open."

A hand-painted sign with "Darla's Diner" perched over a small building with a red and white checkered awning. The huge plate glass windows sent bright orange light out onto a truck and car parked in front. A couple sat in a booth near the doors, sharing a shake with two straws and two older guys sat on stools at the counter, clouds of cigarette smoke creating a halo around them as they shoveled food into their mouths.

"I think Andy's found his people." Grant glanced over at me as he pulled into the parking lot the diner and motel shared. "We should get checked in first."

He reached over to take my hand. "How are you doing? You've been awfully quiet for the last few hours."

I attempted a smile. "I'm fine. Just tired. And worried."

"We'll get you into the room and you can get some rest." He squeezed my hand.

My stomach growled, too. "Actually, food sounds really good."

"Are you sure?"

I nodded at him. "Yeah."

"I'll check us in and meet you over there," Tristan offered. "Drop me off here."

"I'll come with you," Andy said. "It looks a little sketch to me."

Grant stopped the car and let the boys out. The doors slammed and they stood, stretching in the early morning hours, their breath hanging in the frigid air. The pink vacancy sign cast them in a warm glow as they turned and headed into the front office. A balding man greeted them with a yawn.

"Now, food," Grant said, parking in a space near the diner.

I climbed out, glad to finally be out of the car. I twisted my back to release the tension. It didn't work and I reached up absently to grasp the locket. Giving it an experimental tug, I wasn't surprised when it clung to my skin. Scared, but not surprised. Then, Grant's hand was on the small of my back and he guided me through the door of the diner. The smell of bacon brought with it a flood of emotion and I took a deep breath, concentrating on putting one foot in front of the other as I followed Evie to a table in the corner.

She grunted as she moved into the corner booth and slid to the middle. I sat and slid in next to her and Grant next to me, his leg pressed against mine. It was a comforting feeling and I choked down the dread that was growing in the pit of my stomach.

"Are you okay?" he whispered.

"She's being drained," Evie answered, moving the sugar packet bowl and salt and pepper shakers to the side. "It's the locket. It can't be easy carrying a weight like that."

I stared at her for a minute. "How do you seem to know exactly how I'm feeling all the time?"

She shrugged one shoulder and disappeared behind her menu. The bell on the door dinged and Andy and Tristan came in. Grant waved them over and they slid into the booth on Evie's other side.

"All checked in?"

"Yeah," Tristan said, handing Andy a menu, "the guy even gave us a break on the room since we're checking in so late."

"You mean this isn't the type of place that charges by the hour?" Evie said from behind her menu.

"What can I get y'all to drink?" The server stood at our table, her bright green state fair T-shirt announcing the entertainment line-up for this year and a grease-stained nametag with the name Pam printed in careful block letters clinging to it.

"I'll take a coffee," Grant said. "Cream and sugar, please."

"Me, too," I mumbled. I glanced around the diner as Andy and Tristan ordered iced teas, sweetened and unsweetened respectively. Something tugged at my attention. The two guys at the counter weren't causing it. *What is it?* I looked over to the front. The couple had finished their shake and were standing up to go, the girl leaning into the guy's arm as they went out the front door. The feeling didn't leave with them.

"And for you?"

I shook my head and tried to focus on my menu. "Um, I'll have what he's having," I said, pointing to Andy.

Pam raised her eyebrow and looked at me for a moment before writing something on her pad and walking away. I stared at the leg of her jeans as she walked. There was paint on them. Faded yellow and orange. I blinked my eyes.

"It's her," Evie said quietly.

"What's her?" I asked.

"There was a spike over the diner."

"She's not a ghost," Andy said. "At least, she'd better not be because I need someone to bring my food."

I blinked, focusing my energy, or at least what was left of it, on the area around me. From behind me, I heard the sound of a child playing. I turned around in my seat, my knees sinking into the bench cushion.

"Hi," I said to the little boy.

He stopped pushing his truck along the tabletop and looked up at me with the biggest brown eyes I'd ever seen.

"What's your name?" I asked.

He stared at me for another moment and then went back to playing.

I shrugged and turned around in my seat.

Pam dropped off the drinks and then went over to bus the table the young couple had vacated. A bell rang in the back and she disappeared.

"So, I know we should be used to this stuff by now, but it's pretty cool when we get to see you in action," Andy said as he sucked down half his glass of tea.

I furrowed my brow.

Grant leaned over and said in a low voice, "There's no one in the booth behind us."

His words slammed into me. I turned around and looked again. The top of the little boy's head was leaned over the table as he ran the truck back and forth with a quiet, "Pblt, pblt, pblt," noise.

I took a deep breath. "He's a ghost."

"Yep."

"What's he doing here?" I glanced behind me again.

"Can't you talk to him?"

"He won't say anything."

Evie folded and refolded her napkin. "Maybe he can't."

Pam returned to our table, plates lined up and down her arms. She placed them all in front of us and went back to the kitchen for more. When she dropped off the last load, she looked at the table. "You all need anything else?"

"Do you have any kids?" Andy asked.

"What are you doing?" I hissed.

A dark cloud passed over Pam's face. "Um, no. I don't have any kids. If you all need anything else, let me know." She started to walk away.

"Did you have a little boy?" I asked.

Pam stopped, her shoulders rising and then settling. She turned. "I don't know what you all are playing at, but stay out of my business."

When she left, Evie leaned in over the table. "Did you see her eyes? We touched on a nerve."

I nodded and nibbled on a strip of crispy bacon. My mind was blurry with lack of sleep and worry.

"I managed to get this," Andy said. He held up her order pad.

"I don't think that's a good idea," I said. My stomach shifted uncomfortably and I swallowed the bacon as Andy flipped through the slips of paper.

"Is this him?"

I looked up at the photo taped to the inside back cover. In the picture, the same little boy from the booth behind me stared out at me. His smile was crooked. I stared at those dark brown eyes and tried to concentrate on the feeling in the air. I nodded. "It's him."

"She's coming back," Grant whispered.

Andy closed the holder and placed it on the corner of the table as Pam came over with a pitcher of tea. She refilled Tristan's glass. The folder on the table caught her attention and she pushed it back into her apron.

"What happened to him?" Andy asked. "The little boy in the picture?"

Pam stared at us hard for a moment, her jawline working.

"You have paint on your jeans," I said quietly. "He was finger painting the last time you saw him." It was a stretch and I knew it, but I wanted to get her talking.

She glanced down at her jeans and rubbed a hand wistfully over the paint stains. "I yelled at him for getting paint on my new pants. I yelled at him before I left for work and never got to see him again." Her voice shook and she cleared her throat. "That was four months ago. The police say I shouldn't give up hope...but sometimes it's hard, you know?" Suddenly, Pam didn't look like a hardened waitress at a local dive. She looked like a scared young mother. Someone who was scared that her little boy was dead.

I swallowed again, the bacon I'd eaten fighting its way back up. *I don't want to tell her.*

She deserves to know.

I can't.

Andy looked at me for a moment longer then turned to Pam. "What's his name?"

She smiled. "Duncan. He's named after his granddad."

"Do you have anything of his?"

She blinked a few times to clear the tears. "You mean, besides his picture?"

"A truck," I said. "He liked to play with a truck." I glanced behind me. "It's, um, orange, with a missing wheel on the back."

Pam stared at me. "H-how did you know that?"

"She can see things sometimes," Evie said by way of explanation. "Do you know where that truck is?"

Pam nodded. "It's in my purse. I take it everywhere with me so I can give it to him when we find him." She blinked again. "Let me go get it."

"This doesn't feel right," Tristan said. He pushed his plate away.

"She needs to know," Andy said.

"Why are you the one to decide that?"

"He's right." Grant caught Tristan's gaze. "You would want to know, wouldn't you, if it was your family?"

Tristan seemed to think on it for a minute. He sat back in the booth and shook his head. "Do whatever you think is best."

"Isn't this what we've been trying to do in Culvers Grove?" Evie said quietly. "The *whole time.* All we've tried to do is help people. Now, we have a chance to truly help someone and I, for one, think we should take it." She looked at me. "I think we can help her, St. Louis."

I stared at her for a long time. Finally, I nodded. "We can help her."

Pam came back carrying the truck. She handed it to Andy reverently.

Get anything?

He nodded. "Yeah," he breathed. "He's playing with it on green carpet. SpongeBob is playing in the background."

"It's his favorite show." Pam squatted and rested her arms on the tabletop, her chin on her hands and her eyes wide. "That's in our living room."

"There's a knock on the door. He says he'll get it. Someone calls out to wait, but he doesn't listen."

"My mom. She said she was washing dishes in the kitchen when it, um, when it happened."

"He smiles when he opens the door. It's a man, um, tall, black hair. Duncan reaches up to give him a hug and the man takes him toward a car. Blue. Dent on the front fender. Duncan's screaming that he wants his truck, but the man puts him in the car and they're gone. A woman is rushing outside, drying her hands on a towel. She's calling out for him."

Pam's nostrils flared. She stood up and drove her fist into the tabletop. "I *told* the police he took him!" She paced in a small circle, her hands clenching and unclenching at her sides. "They said he wasn't a suspect after questioning him, but I knew it. I *knew* it!"

The two men at the counter looked over.

"Who was the man?" Evie asked quietly.

Pam's eyes sparked. "Duncan's daddy. We moved all the way from West Virginia to get away from him after he broke my jaw. I *knew* it!"

"Everything all right there, Pam?" one of the old men asked, his voice gravelly with concern.

"It was Robert! He took Duncan!" She turned to Andy and reached over the table to grab his hands as they held the truck. "Where is he? Where's Duncan now?"

Andy shook his head. "I, uh, I don't know. But, I need to tell you something, um," he looked up at me hopelessly, the color drained from his face.

I took a deep breath. "Pam, I'm really sorry, but Duncan isn't coming home."

CHAPTER 7

Everyone in the diner moved around me as I sat in the booth. My entire body hurt, inside and out, and I closed my eyes, completely drained. Voices came through as if they were struggling through a layer of cotton to my ears and I rested my chin on my clasped hands. Someone was supposed to call the police. The two men were going to take Pam to the station. She was angry and sad. So sad. Her emotions washed over me, coating me with despair. A hand caressed the back of my neck and I looked over to see Grant in the booth seat next to me.

"You did the right thing," he said quietly.

"Then why do I feel so awful?" My voice hitched. *This wasn't how it was supposed to feel.*

"Anderson?"

I turned, my head swimming with the motion.

Andy tilted his head toward Pam.

She stood at the edge of the table, streaks of tears covering her cheeks. She swallowed. "Can you tell me where my little boy is?" Her voice was small and her eyes peered out at me from a depth of sadness I hadn't seen in a long time.

Trepidation freezing me to the spot, I shook my head. *All of those people I haven't helped. All of those ghosts stuck in the same place for eternity. Never moving on...never being with their loved ones...never finding peace.* Tears pricked my eyes as I stared at Pam. *I can't do this.*

Suddenly, there was another voice in my head. *Sure, you can, Anderson. You have to try at least, right?*

I glanced back at the table behind ours where the little boy sat, running an imaginary truck back and forth across the Formica tabletop. Sighing, I nodded to Grant. He got out of the booth and offered his hand to help me slide out. I walked over to the table behind me on shaking legs, Grant's arm around my middle for support. I slid into the booth opposite the child and leaned down to catch his eye.

"Hi, Duncan. My name's Marissa and I want to try to help you." I heard Pam gasp audibly. My gaze didn't waver as his baleful brown eyes stared at me.

"Truck," he said, his little mouth drawn up in a pout.

"Duncan, can you tell me where you are? What do you see around you?"

He shook his head. "Truck."

"His truck," I said, holding out my hand without breaking my gaze. I felt the hard metal object placed lightly in my palm. Bringing it around to the table, I placed it, wheels down on the surface.

Duncan's face lit up and he grabbed at the toy. Sparks arced around it as his fingers made contact with the metal. The toy shimmered and then became a bit less *here.* He moved it across the table, making a vroom-vroom sound with his lips.

"Where did it go?" Pam whispered.

I cleared my throat, disappointment clouding my vision. *He's not going to talk to me.*

It's okay, Anderson. There's something more to do, that's all.

Pushing away the feeling of hopelessness, I took a deep breath. "Duncan, can you tell me where you are? What you see around you?"

Duncan looked up at me, a quizzical look in his eye. "Trees. I'm cold."

"Can you see anything around you besides trees?"

He thought for a moment. "I see water. There's a hill and I can see a big white bubble on sticks."

I relayed this information to Grant.

"A water tower?" he offered.

"Is it a big white water tower, Duncan? Does it have letters at the top? Can you see them?"

He squinted and looked up at the ceiling of the diner. "Mmmhmm."

"He can't read," Pam whispered.

I shook my head to clear it. "Duncan, can you see the letters on the top? Can you tell me what they are?"

He smiled at me, his tongue pushing through the space where his two missing teeth vacated. "I can read it," he said proudly. "It says 'Duncan.'"

I sat back into the booth hard and blinked back tears. I wasn't going to be able to help this family. How on earth were they going to find his body with the only clues of a wooded area, a lake, and a water tower? Hundreds of locations would fit the criteria. I sat back in the booth and swept a hand over my eyes.

"What'd he say?" Pam gasped. "What letters does he see?"

I finally looked over at her. She was surrounded at this point by everyone in the diner and they were all leaning close, expectant eyes bearing down on me. I cleared my throat again. "He said it says his name. I'm sorry, Pam." *I can't help him.*

Something more. There's something more...

What? I felt exhaustion pulling at me.

I don't know.

Pam stared at me. "Duncan. We passed through a Duncan, West Virginia on our way out of MacFarlan when we left Robert. Duncan, h-he was so excited when we saw that tower! He said they must've known he was coming and painted it special for him!" She grabbed me and wrapped her arms around my shoulders. "Thank you so much," she whispered against my neck.

"Mommy?"

Pam's head shot up and she looked across the table. "Duncan? I heard Duncan!" she practically screamed. "Duncan! Mommy's here! Mommy's here!" Tears streamed along her face as she laugh-cried.

"Here," I said, placing my hand out on the table, palm up. "Take my hand."

Pam sat next to me and placed her cold hand in mine. Her breathing was uneven and shallow and I caught whiffs of bacon from her clothing mixed with the acrid scent of despair from her soul. I placed my other hand on the table.

"You're not strong enough for this," Evie whispered.

I looked up at her. "I have to try." I turned back to Duncan. "Take my hand, Duncan."

He started to reach out, but his hand paused a bit above mine. He stared at me for a moment. "Why?"

"Your mommy wants to talk to you."

Duncan yanked his hand back and held it against his chest. "Mommy's mad at me."

"What's wrong? Is he still here?" Pam asked. Her voice held an undercurrent of panic in it.

I turned to look at her. "He says that you're mad at him."

Pam dropped her gaze. "I'm not mad. Tell him I'm not mad." She squeezed my hand for emphasis.

"Duncan, your mommy's here with me and she told me that she's not mad. She wants to talk to you."

He regarded me from his sullen position on the booth seat. "She's not mad?"

I shook my head. "She's not."

He sat up and reached out his hand. This time, he made contact with my palm. Light shot through me from both hands, running up and down my arm in waves of electricity.

"Duncan!" Pam cried. "Duncan, it's me, Mommy! Can you see me, Bug?"

"Mommy?" Duncan squinted and leaned in. A wide smile broke across his face. "Hi, Mommy."

"Hi, baby!" Tears ran down Pam's face as she laughed. "Bug, I'm so sorry I yelled at you. I'm not mad, I promise!"

He furrowed his little brow. "You're not?"

"No, baby. I'm not mad. See? I'm wearing the jeans with your painting on them. They're so pretty!"

He relaxed. Something seemed to catch his attention and he looked away.

"What is it, baby?"

He turned back toward her, a huge smile on his face. "Mommy! It's Duke! I see him! He wants to play, Mommy. Can I go? Please?"

Pam's face fell. "Y-you see Duke?"

"Yes, Mommy! Can I please go play with him? I miss him so much!"

I was close to losing it. My grip on their hands was weakening and I could feel the muscles in my arms shaking with the effort.

Pam wiped at the tears with her free hand. "Yes, Bug, you can go play with him."

His energy began to pull away. "Bye, Mommy!" From a distance, I could hear his voice, overlaying the one I could hear nearer to me. "Hey, Duke! I missed you!" There was a distant bark in response.

"He's going," I managed to choke out.

Pam squeezed my hand, the electricity passing through in a flood now. I felt it cross through my chest, an infusion of pure love, before it passed into my other arm to his hand.

He looked back at her and smiled. "I love you, too, Mommy."

A moment later, his hand pulled from mine. I heard laughter and closed my eyes.

Check it out, Anderson.

I forced my eyelids open and looked up. Duncan hovered above us. It looked like he was running, chasing something, and he was laughing. The sound was pure and wonderful and filled me with a peace I never wanted to let go.

"Do you see it?" I whispered to Pam.

She, too, was staring up at the ceiling of the diner. "Yes, yes, I see him."

For a moment, he circled above our heads and then, he shot up and out through the ceiling. Andy and Evie ran outside while Grant and Tristan duck-walked me outside into the parking lot. Pam and the two men followed.

We looked up, watching as Duncan's form dissolved into millions of brilliant points of light, cascading and spiraling into the column that rose into the sky. The clouds exploded with veins of lightning.

Then, all was quiet. Still.

Pam turned to me, her eyes glistening in the neon. "I don't know how you did that..." Her chin quivered and she blinked several times. "Thank you."

My chest heaved as I gulped the frigid air. I tried to speak, but nothing came out.

"You're welcome." Grant took Pam's hand for a moment and squeezed it. "We're sorry about Duncan."

She nodded, and then turned as a pickup truck driven by the old men pulled up next to us.

"Hey, Pam! Come on. You're gonna' freeze out there." One of the men pushed open the passenger door. "We'll take you over to the sheriff's office."

Pam looked once more at me and then turned to get into the truck. The door slammed and then the truck was gone and our little group was left in the middle of the parking lot, the buzzing neon sign casting us all in an unearthly glow.

Grant hugged me. "You good?"

I tilted my head a fraction of an inch. "Um, yeah?"

He looked down at me and I pulled away from him.

"Yeah, I mean, I feel better than I have in a long time." A grin spread along my features, stretching my cheeks with the unfamiliarity of the action. There hadn't been a lot to smile about in the last few months. I blinked and shook my head, finally releasing the fog that had clung to me like a disease. My legs felt strong and true and I tested them, leaning my weight from one side to the other.

"I-I feel great?" I looked up at my friends.

Why do you sound so surprised? Andy raised an eyebrow in my direction. *We finally got to help someone.*

"This was the way it was always supposed to be," I whispered.

You're wrong, Marisssaa.

I shook my head, willing the unfamiliar voice to leave me alone. Leave me with this small victory. Leave me with a win. If only for a moment.

CHAPTER 8

The room wasn't as bad as the outside had led us to believe, and after taking turns in the small bathroom, we were all ready for bed in less than an hour. Evie pushed the two armchairs together against the footstool and made herself a pallet on top. We each donated a pillow from our beds and then climbed under the covers. The heater hummed happily from its space under the green curtains. The warm air filled the room and my eyes grew heavy as the weight of the comforter pressed down on me. Grant's hand rubbed my arm, the monotony of the motion lulling me into complete relaxation.

He spoke as I was drifting. His voice brought me back to the world and I rolled over toward him.

"What?" I mumbled. My eyelids fought my effort to open them.

"I asked if you were ready for whatever we find in Savannah. We'll be there tomorrow."

I sighed, the gravity of our journey jolting me full of adrenaline and I sat up, bringing my knees to my chest. Grant sat up next to me and pulled the blanket over my knees.

"We're heading in blind, aren't we?" I whispered. I shook my head. "I don't know what I'm supposed to do and everyone's following me into battle assuming that I'm leading the charge." I shrugged. "I don't know what I'm doing."

You never do.

I leaned around Grant and glared at the lump on the other bed. "Go to sleep."

The lump shifted and Andy sat up. "Not tired."

"Neither am I," Evie said from under her covers.

"It's almost three a.m." Tristan growled, pulling the covers off Andy and over his own head. "Go to sleep."

"I can't," Evie said, her voice muffled.

"This is ridiculous." I leaned over and turned on the lamp.

Tristan groaned from inside his cocoon.

Andy patted his leg. "You'll be fine. Anderson, what's the plan?"

I shook my head. "I wish I knew a little more about what we were dealing with." I looked meaningfully in his direction. *You up for a reading?*

Andy smiled and transferred his lanky frame onto our bed. Evie brought over a blanket and sat, too, the corner of the mattress sinking.

"You guys are going to try to read the locket?" Grant asked. He looked around at our faces. Then, he nodded resolutely. "You guys are going to try to read the locket."

I scooted forward and moved my shirt collar down. The locket was embedded in my skin, the chain hanging loosely around my neck.

"Um, Anderson, have you looked in a mirror lately?"

I blinked and took a deep breath. "I know."

Grant grasped my shoulder and turned me toward him. "Oh, my God."

"It's not that bad," I said under my breath.

"Not that bad?" He stared at me, a million emotions passing through his gaze in quick succession. "There are green and purple veins spreading out from it."

"Does it hurt?" Evie asked.

I shook my head. "Not much. It's more like a dull thud now." I jutted my chin out. "I can handle it."

Grant reached out and grasped the locket. He pulled a bit, his teeth gritted against the burning. The locket glowed and his body grew rigid. He opened his mouth, gulping air.

I placed my hand over his. "Please don't. It's not going to work."

He nodded and took his hand back, the worry in his eyes deepening as he cradled his hand against him.

"Andy?" I put my hair into a loose bun and sat up straight.

He nodded and reached out, his fingers closing around the edges of the locket. He winced. *It's hot.*

Then you'd better get to work.

Andy nodded and closed his eyes. I followed suit. Images immediately began to swim in front of me, spinning and distorted.

"Concentrate," I whispered.

"I-I don't know which one to grab onto."

Evie's voice was quiet. "Find the point where they were together. One memory."

I opened my eyes and stared at Evie.

She shrugged. "It makes sense, right? If Jacob was her father, then there was a point where they shared a memory, right?"

I shook my head. "The letter said that he never met his daughter."

"Then go back further. Back before his daughter."

"To Charlotte?"

She nodded.

I blinked and closed my eyes. *You heard her.*

Andy took a deep breath. "I see Martin. He's putting the locket in the nightstand with the note. Now, he's playing with your grandma. They're in the forest and they're playing tag. She's laughing and so is he." Andy paused.

"Go back further," I prompted. I watched as Andy filtered through time, stretching the memory out like taffy. "There," I said. "Stop there."

The image of a boy shoveling dirt into a grave in a field passed into my consciousness. "Who's that?"

"What do you see?" Evie asked.

I described the scene to her. "Can you get closer?" I asked Andy.

A swooshing sound and we moved toward the boy. He looked to be around thirteen and was tall with unkempt brown hair poking out from under his straw hat. Andy moved us around to get a better view. The boy's face was covered in dirt but there were two streaks where his tears had cut through. He stopped digging for a moment and leaned against the shovel, taking his hat off to brush a sleeve across his forehead.

I peered into the hole and pressed my lips together. A body lay shrouded in a white cloth, covered partially in loose dirt.

"Who is it?" I whispered.

"Look here." Andy shifted my perspective and I found myself tilted, looking at a cross that was made from sticks lying near the pile of dirt. The initials "M. S." were scratched into the wood and below that a date: 1823.

"Do you think this is Martin's grave?" I opened my eyes and looked at Andy.

"Then, that's Henry burying him," Tristan said from under his covers.

I squinted and looked at the boy's features. "It could be. Andy, can you go back further?"

In response, the image faltered and then sped away, other images replacing it in quick succession. The images spun back and then sprung forward.

"No, go back," I said.

Andy's hand trembled on my chest. "I'm not doing this," he said. "It's like someone else has control of the visions."

"Martin," I breathed.

The images slowed and then stopped on the interior of a small cabin. A fire burned in the stone hearth and the curtains were drawn, the entire room filled with gloom and sadness. A boy sat at the table, his head buried in his hands. It was Henry. A hacking, sick cough rose up from the bed in the corner and the boy stood up and rushed to the bedside.

"Who's in the bed?" Grant asked.

I described the room, as we got closer to the bed. In it was a woman. Her brown curls were piled loosely on top of her head and her eyes were bright with fever. I moved a step closer. "It's...the woman I saw in the cavern. The woman Martin changed into."

Henry stepped closer to the woman and put an arm around her back to support her as she coughed into a handkerchief. When she finally stopped hacking, she brought the cloth away from her face and stared at the blood.

Henry's eyes filled with tears. "Mama," he croaked out.

"Shhh," the woman whispered before falling into another bout of coughing. When she recovered, she reached up to grasp onto Henry's arm. "You must never speak of me as such. Make me this promise," she hissed.

Henry nodded.

"Should she ever find me, she will kill the both of us. Do you understand?"

"Yes, ma'am," Henry muttered.

She leaned back against the headboard. "When I pass, bury me in the field near the giant pin oak. Tell no one of my passing. As long as no one knows, the money will continue to arrive each month."

"I am sure, if I tell him, that he would..."

The woman leaned up and stared into the boy's eyes. "Tell no one."

The hacking sound wound its way up through her throat and she doubled over as the image wavered and faded.

How are you doing? I opened my eyes for a second and looked across the bed at Andy. His face was screwed up in concentration and he was biting his bottom lip.

Fine as frog hair, Anderson.

I ignored the lie and closed my eyes again. The images swung by, slowing as they stopped on the cabin. This time, it was winter. Snow covered the small structure and a plume of smoke rose from the chimney. The sound of chopping wood rang out through the valley, echoing off the groves of trees and masking the source of the sound. I shivered involuntarily as the icy wind cut through me.

Suddenly, the air grew heavy, ominous. The cloudy sky darkened and a screeching built from far away. The sound of the axe stopped. I whipped around, trying to find the source of the terror that was building in my core.

Something's coming.

A moment later, two people crashed through the underbrush at the edge of the forest. Martin and a small boy ran through the drifted snow, sending the fine powder up in a sparkling mist around them. The young boy tripped and fell and the man stopped to pull him up.

"Come, Henry," he said. "Hurry."

I followed them through the door of the house as they ran in. Henry tossed ashes on the flames in the fireplace as Martin moved the bed to the side. Wind whipped in through the open door, sending snow skittering across the floor. The screeching built outside as the boy mussed the covers and knocked a chair to the floor. The man crouched near the corner of the bed and pulled back the rug. He opened a trap door in the floor revealing a ladder that led into a small room below. The man looked up.

"They're hiding," I whispered. "From what?"

"Come, Henry," Martin said above the din. "Quickly, son."

Henry took one last look around the cabin and pushed a cup onto the floor before descending the ladder. Martin followed, pulling the door down with the rug falling over the top. I peered below the floorboards, taking a moment to allow myself to get my bearings as I did so. It was a disconcerting feeling, like dipping my head into a tub of water. The room was small, and dark. It smelled like the earth.

Martin wound a piece of leather around the latch again and again, tying it to an enormous root that ran through the wall. When he had checked the door several times, he descended the ladder and sat on the ledge that had been dug out. He placed his arm around his son's shoulders and held him close.

"It will be all right," he whispered.

"Mama," Henry whimpered.

"Shhh, son. I will keep you safe."

The shrieking grew, pummeling the house with its strength. I yanked my head above the floorboards and looked around. Snow blew in through the open door and I drew back against the wall.

Something's coming.

I know, Anderson. We're safe. It's only a memory.

I nodded, knowing that he was right, but feeling the terror pull my chest tight. The darkness grew outside, though it had been midday moments before. My shirt clung to my shoulders, the sensation causing my skin to prick with goosebumps. I swallowed, my ears straining to identify the sound that was assaulting my senses.

What is that?

No clue. Holy crap! What is that?

The room spun on its axis and I almost lost my bearings. A moment later, I was on the floor, my stomach reeling. I tasted bile in my throat and bit down on my tongue, focusing on the pain to drive the nausea away. When my eyes focused, I couldn't figure out what I was looking at for the longest time.

It was standing there in the doorway, its empty eyes scanning the room. It was black the entire way through and reeked of evil and dead things. My nostrils flared and I inched back along the floor.

Anderson, it's okay. It can't see us.

I wanted to believe him, but the way the creature turned its head, it looked like it could see directly into my soul. I held my breath as it drew near. The rags it wore dragged on the floorboards, emitting smoke where they touched the surface. I continued to move away from it, the stench rising off its festering skin making me sick. It swept side to side, taking in the seemingly abandoned home, the broken dishes, the overturned furniture, and the snow-covered floor.

As it turned, I held my breath and shoved my head under the floor again. Henry stared up at the ceiling, his eyes wide with terror. Martin sat next to him, his arms around his son, rocking him gently. His lips moved with a silent prayer.

I pulled my head up again. The creature had moved toward the door. I stood up and let out a sigh of relief which caught in my throat and ended as a choking sob as the creature turned back and stared right at me.

Andy!

It tilted its head, a smile playing upon its bubbling lips. The space between revealed a row of tiny sharp teeth and it stared at me, its head undulating in a serpentine motion.

Yeah, so that thing I said about it not being able to see us?

I moved back a step, my back hitting the table as the creature advanced upon me. There was something familiar about the terror associated with it. The waves of nausea hit me over and over again, and suddenly, my mother was standing in front of me.

"Mom?" I choked out her name, tears stinging my eyes.

"Hey, Sweetie. I miss you." She smiled at me, her impossibly green eyes holding my own.

And, here it was. The moment I had dreamed of over and over again. My mom was here. The nausea passed and I was overcome with emotion. Her lavender perfume drifted up at me. My chest expanded and it was hard to breathe.

"Mom, I've missed you, too. Are you all right? Is it nice where you are? Are you happy?"

A tear escaped her eye and wound its way down her cheek as she smiled softly, tilting her head. She reached up, her palm warm against my cheek. I closed my eyes and leaned into her touch. The smell of her hands. The gentleness of her touch. The all-encompassing feeling of love.

"Let it in, baby girl. It's easier that way."

Something in the air shifted and I opened my eyes. My mom was there, but this time, something was off about the way she looked at me. Something sinister behind the smile in her eyes. I felt pressure against my chest and looked down. Her fingers were fixed around the locket, pulling it toward her. The pain was immediate and searing as the locket began to come loose from my skin. Mom opened her mouth in a smile and I saw rows upon rows of pointed teeth glistening with saliva. I made a mad grab at the locket and managed to get my hands on it, around it, holding it closed as I held it against me with all my might.

Andy! Help me!

There was no answer.

I was alone. Well, not entirely. My mom was here with me. The thought comforted me for a moment more until I heard the screeching noise whirring around me in the cabin. My mother's features melted, revealing the monster beneath. It pulled at the locket with hands that had turned to a black smoky mist. As it pulled, the locket began to glow with a purple light along the edges.

I clamped my hands over it. The pressure intensified and I could feel myself beginning to lose grip on both the locket and consciousness. The drain was swift and absolute. The locket was almost ripped from my fingers. I cried out, using the last of my strength to hold onto it. The creature grabbed hold of the chain and I felt it rip through my fingers, tearing the skin open as the creature pulled one last time, then whipped around and out the door. The snow swirled in its wake and I fell to the floor, the locket burning my chest.

Then, the shrieking stopped and the sky lightened.

I let my head fall, my forehead resting on my arm. Blood ran warm on my chest from the scratches and my fingers felt like they were on fire.

"I do not know..."

"She very well may have saved us..."

"Get the bed made up..."

"Wood on the fire..."

The voices behind me held my attention for a moment and then the seductive call of sleep – of a release from this anguish – won out, and I closed my eyes.

CHAPTER 9

The first thing I felt was a coolness on my chest. My eyelids fluttered open and my nostrils were assaulted by a spicy odor. I looked down and saw a white cloth covering my chest above the neckline of my shirt. I blinked several times and brought my hand up so I could look at my fingers. Though they were still smarting, the pain was duller and more manageable. I blinked a few more times and cleared my throat. My mouth was dry and my tongue stuck to the roof. Struggling to sit up, I saw the man and boy sitting in righted chairs at the table, deep in conversation. A fire flickered in the fireplace. A lantern sat on the table, its light moving and stretching the shadows along the walls of the small cabin.

"What was that thing?" I asked, my voice scratchy.

They both turned and the man stood up. He approached the bed and leaned to look at the wound under the cloth.

"It will hurt," he said, placing the cloth back, "but it will heal."

"Mama taught me how to put camphor on it," the boy said proudly from his perch on the chair.

The man threw him a warning look and the boy wilted, his lips pressed together.

"Martin?" I whispered.

The man looked at me through guarded eyes. "Who are you?"

"My name is Marissa and I'm your descendant. I'm trying to find Charlotte. To stop her."

Martin's face clouded. He took a step back from the bed and shook his head.

I went on. "I know that you died and told Henry not to tell anyone." I shook my head. "I-I mean, you're going to die and tell Henry not to tell anyone."

"You're going to die?" The boy version of Henry got up from his chair and ran over to the bed.

Crap.

"No, Henry. It's not for a long time. Your mama is fine."

"How do you know all of this?" Martin put a hand on his boy's shoulder and drew him close.

"I'm in a, well, a vision right now. We're looking at something that happened in the past."

"We?" Martin's eyes darted to the door.

"No, I mean, it was Andy and me. Um, so Andy was being eaten by this smoke thing and I pulled it out of him, but when I did, some of me passed into him and now he can see the pasts of objects. It's like Evie, after I bridged her spirit and body, she could see disruptions in the fabric between worlds." I bit my bottom lip. "None of this is making sense, is it?"

Martin blinked and patted Henry on the shoulder. "Why don't you get your book and go read, huh? We can talk about your favorite animal later."

Henry smiled and ran to the fireplace. He hopped up on the hearth, reached up to grab a book from the mantle, and settled himself in a corner near the warmth of the fire. Martin motioned for me to follow him to the table. I got up from the bed and made my way slowly to the table, my legs not yet working properly. He offered me a chair and then a cup of water. I took a sip and waited for him to sit across from me.

Martin lowered himself into a chair and sat there, regarding me. "You may call me Mattie," he finally said. He took his hat off and a cascade of brown curls spilled out onto his shoulders. The hair softened the features of the face and I could see a woman beneath the ruddy cheeks and pronounced chin.

"Mattie." I cleared my throat. A moment of silence passed between us. I squirmed in my chair and considered what else to say.

Mattie spoke first. "We, Henry and I, are accustomed to seeing those like you."

"Like me?"

"Spirits. Those from the other side."

I blinked. "I'm not a ghost."

"We will attempt to help you, to guide you through."

"Hold on, seriously. I'm not a ghost." I shook my head. "I'm here because we need to know what's in Savannah."

Mattie's face darkened. "Only bad memories."

Something tugged on my middle and I looked down. Nothing was there. "Is Charlotte in Savannah?" The tugging sensation came again, stronger this time.

Come on, Anderson! Wake up!

Mattie stared at me. "Charlotte?"

"Your mother."

She blinked several times. "My mother died many years ago."

"I know, but we think she's reaching out, um, pulling people into a locket." I knew I sounded ridiculous, but the insistent pressure at my core could no longer be ignored.

"A locket?"

I reached up and removed the bandage from my chest a bit. My skin smarted and I felt blood gush from the wound.

Mattie leaned over and stared, recognition passing through her features. "My mother told me of a locket. A wedding gift to my father. She said it was cursed. I did not think it was real."

I placed the bandage gently over the wounds and leaned back onto the pillow. Tears stung my eyes. "It's real. You will find it in Culvers Grove and keep it from hurting others. But now," I looked down, "now, you're inside it."

And, you should be, too. Let it in.

Closing my eyes for a moment, I took a deep breath. *This makes no sense. You have to slow down and explain it to her.* I steeled myself against the pain and opened my eyes.

"St. Louis!" Evie threw her arms around my neck. Her hair obscured my view of the hotel room, but I caught a glimpse of everyone standing at my bedside through her curls.

"I'm all right," I managed. My cottony tongue clicked against the roof of my mouth. "Water?"

Tristan held out a cold bottle and I pushed myself up to my elbows, Evie hanging on. She finally let go but sat close to me on the bed.

"Thank you," I said, taking the bottle and pouring the cool water into my throat.

"You're going to need these, too," he said, passing me a couple of aspirin.

I took them gratefully and swallowed them with another long draw from the water bottle. Scooting up in the bed, I leaned against the headboard and looked around at my friends. "So, I met Mattie."

"Who?"

"Martin's real name, Mattie."

"What happened to you in there, Anderson?"

I blinked a few times, trying to collect my thoughts. "I-I watched Mattie and her son hide in a secret room in the floor and then this smoky monster appeared at the door of the cabin. It looked like what we saw at the Weeping Bridge, you know, the night Evie got hurt."

"I saw that, too, but then I was pulled out of the memory." Andy's face was stretched tight with worry. *I'm sorry I left you there alone.*

I waved him off. "It wasn't your fault. I think you left when the memory wasn't a memory anymore."

"More words here, Anderson."

"At some point, the monster could, um, *see* me. It knew I was there and it took the form of my mother. I let her get close because I miss her so much and it was so good to see her." I took a settling breath and plunged on. "By the time I realized it wasn't my mother, it had gotten close enough to grab at the locket. It almost got it, too, but somehow I kept hold of it."

"Got pretty cut up in the process, too," Grant said quietly.

I looked down. Gauze covered my chest and I removed it carefully. Angry red welts surrounded the locket. They were oozing blood. Blinking several times, I placed the gauze back over my chest. "Mattie said that she and her son were used to seeing people 'like me' and they were going to help me move on. She also said that her mother told her about a locket that was cursed."

"Cursed?" Evie breathed.

"I got pulled out of the memory, or dream, or whatever that was before I could ask her more about it."

"Wait a minute." Tristan sat heavily on the bed next to mine. "If Mattie is in the locket, then how could you see her there?"

"Because she was a memory," Andy said slowly.

"But, then, how was she able to see Marissa?"

We sat quietly for a moment.

"If this was a memory, then, this already happened." Tristan looked around at us. "Don't you see? If we ask Mattie about the ghost of a girl with a locket being in the cabin that day, she would remember it."

"I don't understand."

From the looks passed among the others, I could see that I wasn't the only one.

Tristan smiled. "See? It means that we're on the right track! I mean, it's our destiny to be on this trip."

Andy sat beside Tristan and patted his leg. "I didn't think you believed in destiny."

Tristan shook his head. "I didn't used to. I mean, I always thought we were making the choices all along, but what if I was wrong? What if our choices only lead us on predetermined paths? What if Marissa was always supposed to do this?"

Silence blanketed the room for a long time.

"Tristan?"

He turned toward me.

"What difference does it make? Whether I was supposed to do this or not?"

His face fell. "I mean, I guess it doesn't mean a whole lot in the grand scheme of things, but isn't it a little comforting? Doesn't it make you feel a little better and a little more like you're on the right track?" He shrugged.

I wasn't sure how it made me feel, but I hated the crestfallen look on his face. "It does, Tristan. Thanks."

He blinked and smiled. "We haven't had a lot to go on so far. It feels nice to have a direction."

I took a deep breath. "Mattie was scared to death of something in Savannah. Something that had her scared hundreds of miles away and years after she left. She was disguising herself as a man to keep herself and Henry safe."

"Charlotte?" Evie asked.

Everyone was quiet for a bit.

Then, Evie spoke again. "Then, it's another thing pointing at us having to stop her. If she and Jacob were working together to hold everyone in Culvers Grove, then, we have to destroy them both in order to break the curse."

"Mattie's in there, though," I said in a small voice. "What's going to happen to her?"

Evie shook her head. No one else offered a suggestion and the silence spread around us, an almost physical presence in the hotel room. I felt the locket against my skin, hot and cold, pulling and pushing, constantly in flux as it burrowed back into its place on my chest. My eyelids drooped.

"She's had enough tonight," Andy said, standing up. "We all have."

Later on, after the lights were turned off and the breathing from the other side of the room had grown slow and even, I was lying on my side, Grant's body warm and strong behind me. He reached up to pull a tendril of hair from my face.

"It was so terrifying to watch what was happening to you and not be able to do anything," he whispered.

His breath sent a tingle along my arms. I snuggled into him and pulled his arm over me. "I can't imagine," I breathed.

"I hate watching you get hurt," he whispered. "And I hate knowing that when we get to Savannah, it's probably going to happen again."

I took a deep breath, the pain in my chest a dull burn.

Let it in. It will all be over soon.

Grant squeezed me to him and I fell into a fitful sleep, the fear of what we were getting ourselves into coloring my dreams with a muddy filter. In one, two brothers rowed out to a desolate island, the black waters lapping at their boat.

THE WIDOW'S LOCKET

"We all end up alone..."

CHAPTER 10

The sun filtered through the space between the green curtains, one of its rays hitting me directly in the face. I stretched and rolled over. Grant was still sleeping and I lay quietly by his side, listening to him breathe. My breath began to mimic his and I felt the air expanding my lungs, breathing deeply and allowing my tight muscles to relax into the mattress. The cocoon of warmth drew me in and I closed my eyes, holding onto the peacefulness of the moment.

"Morning." Grant's voice was gruff. He cleared his throat. "How'd you sleep?"

I tucked my chin down to my chest and chanced opening one eye. "Fine. You?"

He chuckled. "Any night I get to sleep next to you is a good one."

"Good grief. I'd tell you to get a room, but, well," Evie said from her spot on the makeshift couch. She sat up, her curls wildly haloing her face. She smoothed them down and looked at the other bed. "Hey, where's Andy?"

Tristan's sleeping form was buried under the comforter on one side but the covers were pulled down on the other where Andy had slept. The bathroom door was open and he wasn't in there.

"I'm on it." I reached out to Andy. *Where are you?*

It took a few moments. *In the diner. You all should come over. This is crazy!*

"He's in the diner." I pushed myself up into a sitting position and glanced down at my chest. Taking a deep breath, I pulled the gauze away. The scratches had scabbed over and the locket was set deep into my skin. I picked at the edge of it absently with a fingernail.

Grant took my hand in his. "Please stop. Does it hurt?"

"Not really anymore," I lied, then shrugged a shoulder. "I can handle it."

His eyes held mine for a moment, the muscle in his jaw working. Whatever he was going to say, he didn't, and got up instead. "I call dibs on the shower."

Tristan emerged from under the comforter, his hair standing straight up. "What time is it?"

"7:13."

"Ugh!" Tristan swept the covers over his head and disappeared into the bed again.

Evie walked over and sat on my bed when Grant headed into the bathroom. "Hey," she said, her eyes watching me carefully.

"Stop that."

"What?"

"Stop looking at me like I'm going to break. I'm *fine*." I emphasized the last word and drew my knees up to my chest. "Mostly anyway."

Evie sighed and looked across the room. "What's going to happen to us in Savannah?"

"I don't know. Are you scared?"

She rolled my question around for a bit before she answered. "I was scared of my mom. I was scared of the kids at school. I was scared that you and your dad would get tired of me and kick me out. I'm scared that your dad's not going to make it back from wherever he is," her voice caught when she said this and she turned a wary glance my way. "But, most of all, I'm scared I'm going to lose you, St. Louis."

I scoffed. "You're not going to lose me."

We sat in uncomfortable silence for a bit.

"It's hard to come back from a confession like that," Tristan said from under the covers.

"Shut up." I threw a pillow at the lump in his bed.

"You know we have to decide what we're going to do when we get to Savannah," he said, emerging once again from his cocoon.

"Um, no. Right now, we have to decide what we're going to do about your situation up there," Evie said, waving her hand toward his unkempt mop of hair.

I stood up and put on my jeans. "If Mattie's mother, Charlotte, gave her father, Jacob, the locket – the *cursed* locket – then she's behind all of this. She killed Jacob with the locket, pulled him through it and down into the cavern below Culvers Grove where she's kept him."

"But why?"

"What do you mean 'why'?" I asked Tristan.

"You and Andy said that the letter Jacob was reading in the vision was so full of love. I don't understand why she would have wanted to hurt him."

"Maybe because he left her," Evie said quietly. "Maybe he left and she couldn't handle it. Maybe she wanted to destroy him for leaving."

A meaningful look passed between us.

"I don't know. And, I can't see any more unless we look into the locket."

"And we can't do that without Andy."

"Anyone else need the shower?" Grant stood in the doorway, his hair dripping.

"I'm going to take one," Tristan said, throwing back the covers. "You guys go on ahead. I'll meet you at the diner in a few."

"I, um, think I'm going to stay here for a few minutes, too," I said, pulling at the edge of my shirt. "I want to make a call."

"Your dad?" Evie asked.

I nodded. "I need to check in on him."

She grabbed my hand and squeezed before following Grant out the door.

I sat on the edge of the bed and swept my long hair into a messy bun. My phone lay on the comforter, taunting me. I wanted to call, but it was so much easier to imagine Dad hanging out and talking with Melanie, all better. Back to himself. I sat with the little fantasy for a bit, listening to the water running in the shower. Finally, I snatched my phone and looked up Melanie's contact. Pressing my lips together, I hit the number and watched the screen as it dialed. I hit the speaker and waited, the phone ringing once, twice, and a third time before a click.

"Hello?"

"Um, hi, Mrs. Ingalls. It's Marissa." I cleared my throat, trying to keep it from closing up around the lump.

"Marissa! I'm so glad you called! We have been having such a wonderful time here. It's been so nice having someone in this big old house with me again. We made pork chops last night and I think your dad had three before he gave up. I'm so glad they're still his favorite."

"How's he doing?" I blinked rapidly against the tears.

"Well, he's awfully quiet, but then again, he never did say anything that didn't need to be said."

I smiled. "Can I talk to him?"

There was a rustling as she placed something over the receiver. I heard her talking, but couldn't make out the words. Another moment of silence and then my dad's voice.

"Hey, Peanut."

"Hey, Dad. How are you?"

"Mrs. Ingalls made pork chops. I'm going to hang out with Thomas later today." A pause. "When's your mom coming home?"

I bit my bottom lip hard and took a deep breath. "Sounds like you're having a good time, Dad. Listen, I'll be home soon. I miss you."

"Mrs. Ingalls made pork chops."

"I love you, Dad," I whispered.

"He's going to be fine," Melanie said when she came back on the line. "Time is all that's needed sometimes to put things right. You hear me?"

I sniffed. "Yes, ma'am. Thank you for taking care of him while we're gone."

"He loves you, sweet girl, and he's going to come back. Now, you take care of yourself and have fun on your little trip."

I nodded and squeaked out another thank you before hitting the button on the phone. My chest heaved as I tried not to cry.

"It's okay to cry," Tristan said from the doorway of the bathroom where he was buttoning up his shirt. "Let it out a little at a time. If you don't, it'll build up until you feel like you're going insane."

I nodded and let a few tears fall. They made dark spots on the comforter. Tristan crossed to the bed and sat, the scent of budget hotel soap rising up from his skin. He put an arm around my shoulders and pulled me over to lean against him.

"He's going to be fine. We all are."

I sniffed again and let a few more tears fall. Then, I wiped at my eyes. "I promise I'll have a good cry when this is all over and everyone is safe again."

"I wouldn't expect any less from you, Marissa Anderson." He smiled and stood, offering me a hand.

I stood up and slid into my shoes. We packed up our belongings and put the bags in Grant's trunk before heading across the parking lot to the diner.

"Lot more cars here than last night," Tristan mused as we climbed the steps to the door.

The moment the door opened, the familiar scent of bacon hit me in the face. I blinked back tears and thought of my grandma. I wished I could check in on my other family members.

"What the...?" Tristan asked, shaking me from my thoughts.

I looked up and saw Andy sitting at a large table, covered with heaping plates of food. People surrounded him and were handing him things.

Check out my mad skills, Anderson!

CHAPTER 11

What are you doing?

Andy smiled and pushed a chair out with his foot. "Sit down and watch me work."

Grant shrugged and I sat next to him and Tristan sat down next to Evie.

"How's your dad?" Grant asked, leaning in to my side.

I swallowed. "A little better."

He took my hand and squeezed it under the table.

"Can you tell anything from this?" An old man in a John Deere hat handed Andy a glass figurine.

Andy took the item and stared at it. He winked at me and then closed his eyes. "I see a beautiful woman. Her name is Josephine, but you call her Josie."

The old man's eyes glistened. "Yes! That's right."

Andy turned the cat figurine in his hands once more. "You won this for her at a carnival. You were both young then. She thinks of you and smiles every time she dusts it." He turned it once more. "Oh." Andy opened his eyes and his voice grew somber. "I'm sorry she passed away."

The old man took the figurine from Andy and tucked it reverently into the bib pocket of his overalls. "Thank you, son." He pumped Andy's hand with both hands. "This kid's the real deal," he said to the people gathered around.

I took a deep breath. *Don't you think this is a little much?*

What's wrong with it? Makes them feel good to connect with their past and makes me feel good because, well, bacon. He held a piece of bacon out to me. *C'mon. Free bacon. We don't have any money left. It's the only way to eat breakfast.*

I shook my head and rolled my eyes, but took the bacon he offered, my stomach suddenly rumbling. We tucked into a huge breakfast and watched as

Andy read a few more objects before heading out the door.

"There's a bank in the next town over," Tristan told us while Grant filled up the car with gas. "We'll see if they'll cash Evie's check."

I nodded absently and stared out the window at the gathering clouds. They twisted and turned into each other, the gray pressing down on me and matching my mood. I was thinking about my dad and about what he was going through. Why hadn't Evie taken so long to get back to herself? Or Andy for that matter? Evie was down there longer than Dad was. Why was she able to bounce back and not him? Something tugged at the edge of my consciousness. *You already know the answer.* I took a deep breath. It's because Jacob was so much stronger when he took Dad. He did more damage in a shorter time. And, if Jacob was that strong and he was being kept by Charlotte, how strong was she? Well, I didn't want to think about that.

"You haven't said anything since the hotel room," Evie said quietly from the back seat, rousing me from my thoughts. "You all right up there?"

I nodded and then turned in my seat to face her. "Do you think we're going to be equipped to take on someone who could create something so powerful?"

Evie's eyes dropped to the gauze on my chest for a moment, and then held my own. "It doesn't look like we've got much of a choice, St. Louis."

I furrowed my brow. "Something's still bothering me, though. What's going to happen to Mattie when we get Jacob to Savannah?"

Evie shook her head. "Do you think we can get her out?"

I bit my bottom lip. "Not without letting him out."

"Well, that's not an option." Tristan looked up from his phone. "But maybe reuniting the entire family: father, mother, daughter, will fix everything?" he asked hopefully.

I shook my head. "I don't think it's going to be that easy. I feel like we're missing part of the story. Why did Charlotte curse the locket she gave Jacob? And, why did it seem like she loved him in the letter? And why was she taking other souls through the locket? And, why is it taking ghosts if she probably died, like, a hundred years ago? And, why did Mattie disguise herself as a man? And, why is this all tied to Culvers Grove and my family?" I ran out of breath.

"You're gonna hurt your brain, Anderson."

I blinked rapidly. "We don't have any answers!"

Andy reached up from the backseat and patted my shoulder. "Step one; get Evie's check cashed so we have money to make it to Georgia. Step two; get to

Savannah. Step three; set ourselves up in a hotel and get some food and sleep. Step four; follow the locket to Charlotte."

I looked down and gestured toward the passenger window. "It's not pulling toward the east anymore."

Andy snickered.

"What?"

"You've always been crap at directions, Anderson. Wonder what's changed?" He ticked his eyebrow up a notch.

I squinted at him. "It's going to lead me?"

He raised both eyebrows. "Looks like."

Grant got in the car, the frigid air spinning in through the open door. "Sorry," he mumbled, blowing into his hands before starting the car. "What's going on?"

"Hey, Grant, how good is your girlfriend at directions?"

I turned around and sulked in my seat.

Grant tossed a smile in the rearview mirror as he pulled out onto the road to head back to the interstate. "Sorry, babe, you couldn't find your way out of a wet paper bag."

"The bank is three miles to the southeast of our current location," Tristan said from the backseat. "How do we get there, Marissa?"

"Turn left at the next intersection to head north. Then, we'll turn east onto the interstate and then take the exit and head south for a bit before heading east into the town," I instructed.

Grant side-eyed me and then looked into the mirror again. "She right?"

I assumed Tristan confirmed, but I was busy staring out the window at the craggy grass shooting out from a thin layer of snow in the fields along the road. The fact that the locket was somehow using me as a guiding device was unsettling and I didn't know what to do with that information. A moment later, I felt Grant's warm hand rest on my leg. I closed my eyes and took a deep breath.

We were the first to arrive at the bank and got out of the car as a teller was turning the sign to OPEN in the window. The sleepy town reminded me of Culvers Grove. The bank was housed in a squat building with a rock edifice and a flat roof. We walked in and watched as Evie signed the back of the check. She took it to the bank teller and handed it over while we gathered around.

The woman behind the counter regarded Evie with a bored expression. "ID," she requested, holding out a bony hand through the small gate across the space in the counter.

Evie dug in her purse and presented her driver's license.

"Account number?"

"I, um, don't have a checking account."

The lady looked up again and almost rolled her eyes. "Sorry," she said, sliding the check back to Evie. "We can't cash an out of state check in this amount. I suggest finding a Wal-Mart and cashing it there."

"Gee, thanks for nothing," Evie said, her cheeks flushing as she shoved the check and her ID back into her purse.

"We'll look for something further up the road." I took her elbow and guided her toward the front doors. The guys went out before us and held the doors open.

Suddenly, Evie spun around, breaking my hold on her elbow and faced the teller.

"You know, you ought to leave him. It's not going to get better. Believe me, it only gets worse." With that, she turned on her heel and headed through the open doors.

I caught the surprised look the teller gave before I followed my friend out to the car.

"What was that?" I asked after we started moving again.

Evie waved a hand. "Her color was muddy and scared."

"You can still see them?"

She nodded, her curls moving with the motion. "Since I've been around you so much lately, they're starting to come back a little." She swept her hair out of her eyes. "Besides, she'd tried to cover up the bruises on her face with makeup. It never worked for my mom either."

We sat in silence for a bit as Tristan gave directions to the nearest Wal-Mart to Grant. After a quick trip to the check cashing counter, we bought a few supplies and then headed back to the car. It was an eight-hour drive to Georgia and we were all itching to get there. When I got back to the car, I curled up under Grant's bomber jacket and closed my eyes, the humming of his tires on the asphalt lulling me into a state of semi-consciousness. I used to love that space when I wasn't quite awake or asleep. I used to lie in my bed when I was a little girl and stare at the ceiling, watching the textured swirls of paint begin to move into shapes. They would turn into fluffy clouds with castles and trees. I would use it as the backdrop to epic plays with my hands as characters. My eyes would open and close, slower and slower, until my eyelids became too heavy to open. Then, I would fall asleep to the sounds of my mom and dad talking in the living room, their voices low and comforting. I was safe.

Marisssa…

The locket burned. My eyes popped open and I looked up again at the clouds. The place I used to love between awake and asleep had turned dark and foreboding. I took a deep breath and stared out the window, determined to stay awake until we reached Savannah.

CHAPTER 12

We drove all day, stopping only for gas and gas station meals along the way. Tristan kept up a running history about the city of Savannah from the back seat as we drove. Some of the information hit my brain and stuck. Founded in 1733 by James Oglethorpe. Originally twenty-four city squares, now only twenty-two. A fire in 1796 destroyed almost the entire city. A fire and yellow fever killed a tenth of the population in 1820. With each new fact, I imagined more and more spirits wandering the streets.

By the time we drove across the river into Savannah, it had been dark for hours. The locket burned hot for a moment, searing my skin. I gritted my teeth against the pain as a voice rose up from the locket: *Marisssaaaa.* I looked around to see if anyone had heard it, but no one reacted. I placed a hand over the locket and willed it to stay quiet.

Tristan directed us to a hotel near River Street and we pulled into the parking lot. The guys emptied the car and got the bags while Evie and I went into the hotel to get a room.

"How are you now that we're so close?" she asked, her arm intertwining in mine as we walked.

I shrugged. "Not much different, I guess."

"The locket?"

"It feels like there's electricity pulsing through it now." I glanced over at her. "It burns sometimes."

"Is that different than before?"

I nodded, my eyes filling with tears. "It started when we left Culvers Grove."

Evie's brow furrowed as she opened the door for me. "Well, St. Louis, whatever's going to happen, it's going to all be over soon."

"Not sure that makes me feel better."

The front desk clerk looked like he was twelve and didn't bat an eye when Evie told him she was eighteen. Evie paid for two nights in cash including a deposit and we texted the guys and let them through a back door before heading into the elevator. When we got to the room, Tristan dug into his bag and pulled out a handful of granola bars. He tossed one to each of us. Then he and Grant decided to go out for something more substantial.

"You'll be safe while we're gone?" Grant asked me.

I nodded. "I'll be fine. I promise we'll stay here and won't go looking for Charlotte."

"It's not you going to look for her that I'm worried about."

"I'll stay here and protect them," Andy said, flopping down on the couch and turning on the television.

I wanted to get into the shower and wash away all of the grime from the car ride and let the uncertainty and fear wash down the drain as well. The simultaneous push and pull of the locket in my chest terrified me and I didn't know how long I could keep my defenses up against it. I was so tired and part of me wanted to let go.

"I'll be fine," I said again. "Go. Cheeseburger. Lots of fries."

"Diet soda?"

"I don't care, just something with caffeine."

Grant kissed me on the top of my head before he and Tristan headed out. As soon as they left, I shot into the bathroom and locked the door behind me. Turning on the shower, I let the bathroom fill up with steamy warmth while I sat on the toilet seat and let the exhaustion wash over me. Tears fell as I reached to take off my shoes. The electricity pulsing through the locket dulled a bit as I took off my jeans and threw them in the corner. I wiped a hand across the mirror and stared at my reflection. Looking down, I pulled the tape from my skin and the gauze from the locket. My skin had grown up along the edges of it. *It's trying to get in.* Purple and green veins spread out from it, creating a spider web of horrid colors throughout my chest. It looked like a giant, ugly bruise and I stifled a sob.

I turned the water to the hottest it would go and stepped under into the lava-like stream, letting the water wash through my hair, my scalp tingling in the heat.

"Marissssaaaa."

The whisper rose up from the locket on my chest and I clamped my eyes closed, ignoring the pushing sensation. It was a constant pressure now on my ribcage and I felt like I couldn't get a good breath.

It would be easier to let it in.

My eyes flew open and I pushed the curtain back. The bathroom was empty. The voice had come from inside me, though. Like when Andy or my grandma talked to me. I shook my head and poured shampoo from the little bottle into my palm. It didn't suds up very well, but it smelled delicious and I rubbed it into my hair and scalp, spreading the scent around me.

It's going to happen anyway. One way or another, you're going to belong to me.

"Stop it," I whispered. "Just stop, please."

I hurried through the rest of my shower, eager to get back to my friends who could help drown out the voice in my head, if only for a bit. Pressing my lips together, I put on my clothes and concentrated on quelling the insistent thoughts. At this point, I wasn't even sure they weren't my own thoughts anymore. The unfamiliar had become familiar over the past couple of days and I wanted it to go away. Yanking the door open, a cloud of steam followed me out into the room and I saw Evie sitting on the couch, wrapped up in a blanket. The television was glowing blue in the dark room.

I sat next to her and pulled a corner of the blanket over my legs. "Where's Andy?"

"He went to score some extra towels and shampoo bottles." Evie yawned.

We sat watching an infomercial, both of us dozing off several times and jerking awake at any noise. Finally, the door opened and Grant and Tristan came in, plastic bags rustling. Evie got up and turned on some of the lamps while the boys placed the spread on the long dresser. We each grabbed a burger and some fries and began munching.

"Where's Andy?" Tristan asked.

"I'll get him," I said around a mouthful of burger. *Yo, Andy. We've got burgers and fries here.*

Several minutes passed.

"What'd he say?" Grant asked.

"Nothing yet. I'll try again." *Hey, Andy. We'll get shampoo later. Come back to the room.*

Tristan looked over at me. "Is he coming?"

"Why don't you try texting him?"

Tristan sent a text. A bing from the nightstand followed a moment later.

"He left his phone here charging," Tristan said. His voice was uneasy.

The television filled the emptiness of the room while we chewed.

C'mon, Andy. This isn't cool. The mouthful of burger I was chewing suddenly felt too greasy and cold and I spit it into my napkin.

Tristan watched me carefully. "What's going on, Marissa?"

I shook my head again. "I'm sure it's fine, but I'm not hearing anything from him."

"Can you try again?"

Andy, this is not funny. I need you to answer me. Tristan's getting really worried.

Everyone in the room had stopped eating and they were all staring at me. I wiped at my mouth with my napkin. "Evie, where did he say he was going?"

"Um, to look around for extra towels."

Tristan was up and out the door before I could say anything.

"Do we follow him?" Grant asked, jutting his thumb over his shoulder in the direction of the door.

I shoved my feet into my shoes and left my unfinished burger on a napkin on the bed. "Let's go. Everyone, grab your phones. Evie, get a room key."

Grant scribbled a note on the pad of paper for Andy in case he beat us back to the room and tucked it into the space between the door and the jamb as it closed behind us. We headed toward the bank of elevators and Evie shoved the button.

"He went to the main floor," she mentioned as the number rose on the panel above the doors.

I nodded, the feeling of dread spreading icy tendrils of fear along my arms. *Andy?*

Nothing. Radio silence.

We waited for the elevator to lower to the main floor and burst through the doors as soon as they opened. Tristan was at the front counter, leaning over and talking to the desk clerk.

"...looking for our friend. Have you seen him?"

The desk clerk shook his head. "I haven't had anyone come through since you and this guy," he gestured at Grant as we walked up behind Tristan, "came in with food a little while ago."

"Can you check your cameras?"

The desk clerk hit some buttons on the keyboard and watched the screen. "Nope," he said after a few minutes, "only you and this guy leaving and then coming back with food."

"Where's your housekeeping station?" I asked.

"I have some toiletries for guest use here. What do y'all need?"

I shook my head. "No, our friend was going to look for extra towels and we think he might have gone to housekeeping or laundry."

"It's on the valet garage level, but guests aren't allowed down there."

"Can we look?" I asked. "We'll come right back up."

He glanced behind him nervously. "I'm really not supposed to let guests go down there."

"I'm pretty sure you're not supposed to let five people stay in one room or rent a room to someone who's not eighteen, but you've already done both of those things tonight," Evie said. "What's one more?"

The desk clerk took a deep breath and handed us a key card. "Bring it back. My manager will annihilate me if I lose another one."

Evie grabbed the key card from his hand and we practically ran across the lobby to the elevator. The doors slid open immediately and we climbed in. Evie held the card in front of the pad and pushed the G button.

Andy?

Tristan's face was stoic as the elevator slid toward the lowest floor. I reached out and squeezed his arm.

"It'll be fine, I promise," I said. "I'm sure he came down to get towels and probably ended up making a friend or two with the housekeeping staff."

Tristan's lips curled up in a small smile. "He does get along with everybody, doesn't he?"

Andy?

The elevator stopped and the doors slid open. An exit in front of us led out to the garage and a hallway stretched to the left of it. A laundry station hummed behind the first door we came to. Evie used her key card to open it and we walked in, the smell of fabric softener thick in the hot, heavy air. We spread out, looking behind tables and carts for any sign of Andy. Nothing.

My heart beat hard against my chest painfully, sending off electrical pulses from the locket. I gritted my teeth and followed the group along the hallway. Another door said "housekeeping" and Evie knocked. A short man opened the door a crack.

"Excuse me, sir, but we're looking for my friend. We thought he may have come here."

The man opened the door wide. "No one else down here tonight. Buddy was supposed to come in, but he's home with a sick baby. Hopefully, Marta will be able to cover his shift," he mumbled as he closed the door behind him.

I took a deep breath. "Let's think about this logically. There are other entrances and exits from the building. Let's go check them all out and then we'll walk out to Grant's car. If he's not there, we'll head to River Street and see if he's in a restaurant there. He may have followed his stomach, right?"

Evie whispered, "So, why can't he hear *you*?"

I shook my head and tried again. *Andy! Andy!*

"We have to go get our coats," Grant said. "Let's check the room again to make sure he isn't there first."

Tristan nodded and we rode up to the lobby. I held the doors on the elevator while Evie returned the key card to the grateful desk clerk and then we headed back to the room. The note was in the door and nothing had changed when we opened it and stepped inside.

Suddenly, the locket burned hot on my skin and I cried out, the pain knocking the wind out of me for a minute. Grant was by my side, helping me over to the bed. I sat, my legs giving out as I gasped, trying to fight the pressure on my chest. I clawed at the locket, prying it from my chest. Grant's hands were on mine, trying to quiet them.

I spoke and you should have listened. I doubt your friend is as strong as you are.

My throat clenched up and I swallowed a sob.

"I'm going to check the other hallways." Tristan headed toward the door.

I pulled in a deep breath, the pain searing my throat. "Stop, Tristan. We shouldn't go anywhere alone tonight."

"Why not?" He drew himself up and squared his shoulders.

"Because," a tear slipped from my eye, "Charlotte has Andy."

CHAPTER 13

The room exploded with everyone talking at once. I closed my eyes and willed the pain to stop. When it had abated a bit, I opened my eyes and spoke softly. "I'm sorry I didn't tell you, but I think Charlotte's been talking to me through the locket."

My statement was met with silence.

"Wait a minute," Tristan said, "Charlotte's been talking to you? How long, Marissa?" When I didn't answer right away, he shouted his question again. "How long?"

"Since we left Culvers Grove."

"Are you kidding me? How could you not tell us?" He paced in the space between the bed and the closet.

Grant sat next to me on the bed. "How do you know it's Charlotte?"

I blinked back tears and my chin quivered. "I wasn't sure at first. I thought it was Jacob. I mean, it came as part of a dream the first time. But, then it's been happening more and more the closer we got to Savannah." I looked up at Tristan. "I'm so sorry, but I didn't think it was important."

Grant turned my face towards his. "What has she been saying?"

"Things like I should let it in and that she was going to get to me one way or another." My voice was small. "I thought I could handle it."

"Like you're handling the pain?" Evie asked.

I didn't break eye contact with Grant. He looked hurt.

"Why didn't you tell me you were in pain?" he asked.

Anger flared and I snapped. "Well, it's not like anyone can do anything about it! The locket attached to *me*! Charlotte's after *me* because I have Jacob!"

"So, Andy's just collateral damage?"

Grant glanced up. "That's not fair, Tristan."

"Why not? We followed her across the country and now she's telling us that Charlotte is after her?"

"We knew what we were getting into when we came," Evie said.

"But, why Andy?" Tristan stopped pacing and sat on the floor, his back resting against the dresser drawers. "Why him?"

Evie sat next to Tristan. "I think it's because he was able to read the locket."

I cleared my throat. "If Andy was able to tell us what Jacob is saying, she doesn't have the upper hand."

"She's telling you this?" Tristan spat at me, his eyes blazing.

I shook my head. "No, but she said that I should have listened to her and let it in."

"The locket?"

I nodded.

"You've been fighting it since we left Missouri?" Grant's face was drawn tight.

I nodded again. "It wasn't so bad until we got here. I can keep it out, though. I think."

"What happens if you let it in?" Tristan asked.

"No. No way," Grant said. "No way, Tristan."

I placed my hand on Grant's leg. The pain was settling back into a dull pressure. "If I let it in, she has me. It's bad enough now, because I feel like I'm being drawn to her. If I let it in, I think she'll completely control me."

Tristan ran his hand through his hair. "This is crazy. It's my senior year. I should be hanging out at football games and taking trips to tour colleges. Andy and I should be spending our time together before I have to leave." He stared at me. "I shouldn't be in Georgia looking for a ghost!"

"Tristan," Evie began.

"No, he's right," I said. "Tristan, I'm so sorry. I didn't mean for any of this to happen either. You have to believe me."

"I wish you never would have moved to Culvers Grove," he said quietly.

His words stung and I blinked several times. "I don't know what to say here, except that you can leave if you want to. You can go back home. We'll understand. This is too much for anyone to take."

He looked up at me from red-rimmed, glassy eyes. "I can't leave without him," he said.

"Then, we need to figure out what to do next," Evie said.

"For now, though, everyone makes a promise that no one goes anywhere alone, understand?" Grant stood up and flipped the deadbolt on the door. He walked over and checked the windows and then flipped up the bed skirts and checked underneath.

Tristan stood up and walked over to the couch. He sat heavily with his head in his hands.

I moved to the bed closest to him and sat. "I am sorry, Tristan," I whispered.

"I know," he said from behind his hands. "I'm just scared."

"We all are," Evie said as she sat beside me.

Grant coughed and sat on the chair near the window.

"Are you okay?" I asked.

He nodded, but something about his color wasn't right. I leaned against Evie and jutted my chin in her direction.

"He's hiding something," she said.

"What's going on?" I asked.

Grant looked from Evie to me. Then, he sat forward and took a deep breath. "I noticed it when we were in Kentucky, but it's getting worse."

My stomach dropped. "Grant, you're scaring me."

He chuckled. It was a wry sound. "Truth be told, it's kind of scaring me, too."

He leaned into the light cast by the lamp and pushed up his shirtsleeve. There, twisting and turning angrily under his skin were green and purple veins. My hand flew to my mouth and I choked back bile.

"It doesn't hurt," he said quickly. Then, "much."

"How far does it go up?" Evie asked.

He pushed his sleeve up to his shoulder. "Only up to my elbow."

"But that's further than it was this morning," I whispered. "Isn't it?"

He nodded and pulled his sleeve down to his wrist again.

"What happened in Kentucky?" Tristan asked, moving further away from me a bit.

"You touched the locket. Trying to take it off," I said. Tears sprang to my eyes. *It's always him getting hurt. Because of me.*

"And, there's this other thing I've noticed," he said, grabbing my hand and pulling me to my feet.

I looked up as electricity passed through us. The locket burned painfully on my chest and I dropped my hand from his.

"Come on." He headed toward the bathroom.

I glanced over at Evie. She gave me a look that said, *It's not your fault, St. Louis.*

We followed Grant into the bathroom and stood in the doorway. He faced the large mirror that hung on the wall above the sink, the cords standing out on his neck as he leaned forward and squinted at the surface of the mirror.

"What's he doing?" Tristan hissed in my ear.

I shook my head and took a step forward.

"Come look at this," Grant said, not breaking his eye contact with the mirror.

I made my way over to him and stood looking at its surface. "I don't see anything."

"I do!" Evie squealed from the doorway. "How are you doing that?"

"I don't know," Grant replied, his voice steady.

"That's amazing," she said, moving to my side.

I looked back at the mirror and tilted my head. "I don't see anything."

"Me neither." Tristan stayed near the door. "Shouldn't we be…"

"It's like it's reaching right out of the mirror," Evie cut him off. "A spike, St. Louis," she said for our benefit.

"A spike?"

"Yeah, but I can't see where it's coming from."

"Is there a ghost behind the mirror?" I asked.

Grant shook his head with an almost imperceptible move. "I don't think so. There's a room behind the mirror. I think." He shrugged one shoulder. "It's really blurry, but there's definitely something there."

"What's it look like?" Evie asked. "The room?"

"Um, it's got shelves everywhere and there's a fireplace. I think there's someone there, too. It's a figure moving around, but…" He reached up with a hand toward the glass, touching it with a fingertip. The glass moved a bit, ripples spreading out from his finger. I placed my hand over his and brought it back down.

"I just wanted to see if I could," Grant looked over at me, his eyes glassy. He shook his head. "I don't know why I did that." He blinked several times and stood up straight.

"The spike's gone now," Evie said. "Your color's weird, too." A second later, a smile turned her mouth. "You look like St. Louis and her dad."

He raised an eyebrow.

"The colors around you. They're like hers."

"But, he didn't take a part of me like you and Andy," I said. "It doesn't make sense."

"Maybe the locket gave him powers. Maybe he's cursed. Maybe some of your powers came out through the locket." Evie took a deep breath. "All I know is that we need to get the locket back to Charlotte before it kills both of you." She touched my arm and left the bathroom.

Tristan stared at me for a long minute and then went back into the room after Evie.

I gripped the edge of the sink counter and dropped my head. "I am so sorry, Grant," I whispered. "I am so sorry about all of this."

His finger tilted my chin toward him and I lost myself in his earnest eyes. The flecks of color danced as he leaned in and kissed me. Then, he wrapped his arms around my shoulders and held me close. My head moved up and down as his chest rose and fell with his breath. His heartbeat calmed me and, ignoring the electricity and the painful pull on my chest, I let him hold me; let him hold the pieces of myself together for a moment. I would be strong enough in a minute, but I needed this break, this reprieve from the crap-show that had suddenly become my life. In his arms, my dad was home again, joking around over his cup of coffee. Evie was living with us and she was happy. Andy and Tristan were safe and I was with Grant. My safety net. My friend. My boyfriend. My love.

I let myself melt into him for a moment more and then I took a deep breath and stepped away. I pressed my lips together. "Guess you're in this now whether you wanted to be or not."

He smiled down at me. "Well, I wasn't doing anything else this weekend."

"Come on. We have to figure out how to get Andy back."

CHAPTER 14

"That has to be it," Evie said. "It has to be."

I shook my head, trying to clear it. Everyone in the room was moving, preparing to foray out into the dark city streets to find Andy. I sat on the bed, feeling as if I was listening to a joke that I wasn't in on the punchline. "It doesn't feel right."

"What are we going to do when we get there?"

I shook my head again. "I don't know." I pushed the feeling of abandonment down as it tried to rise through my throat again. The last time I'd faced whatever was under the town, I had my whole family and my friends with me. Now, well, now our number had dwindled. I looked up and realized everyone was looking at me. "Um, what?"

"We have to let Jacob out of the locket."

My hand flew up to my chest. "I don't think that's a good idea."

"Think about it, St. Louis. Charlotte wants you to bring her Jacob."

"And what information brought you to that conclusion? And what would happen to Mattie?" I swallowed. "And us?"

"Why did Charlotte take Andy?" she asked softly.

"Because she knew we would come for him," Tristan answered. "Right? It's her ace in the hole. She's holding him hostage to get what she wants."

"Jacob," I whispered. *This doesn't feel right.* I rolled my head on my shoulders to loosen them and leaned back against the headboard, the dull throbbing in my chest taking almost all of my attention to hold away the pain.

"Mattie's been leading us to Savannah since we left Culvers Grove. She's been keeping Jacob from getting to you, right?"

I looked at my chest. The burning was incessant now. "We're trying."

Evie sat next to me on the bed. "When we get there, we open the locket and let Mattie out. Then, we can trade Jacob for Andy."

It's not that simple. I looked at Evie and then at Tristan whose hopeful face peered at me from the couch. *What choice do we have? Andy, if you can hear me at all, I could sure use some advice here. Got any ideas?* I listened intently for a few minutes and then sighed heavily. "We can't keep sitting here all night."

Tristan was up off the couch and packing a bag in one swift movement and Evie got up to help him. Grant sat in the spot she vacated. I appreciated that he didn't hold my hand. Even my being near him now made the burning sensation in my chest intensify.

"You okay?" he asked.

I nodded then looked over at him. "Everything feels off tonight, you know?"

"I know." Grant picked at a spot of mud on his jeans. "I believe in you. Always have. Always will." With that, he stood up and shrugged on his coat. "You ready?"

I closed my eyes, centering my thoughts. "No, but what choice do we have?"

"Lead the way," Evie said as I passed by her to the door.

The elevator ride seemed to take forever. People got on and off at each of the floors. A family with three boys got on in their swimsuits, headed for the pool. The two older boys laughed and joked, shoving each other good-naturedly while the littlest one stood and stared at me, his blue eyes never wavering from mine.

"You're pretty," he said.

I tried to smile. "Thank you."

The doors slid open and the family got off and headed through the lobby. The little boy remained behind, staring at me.

"Ryan! Come on!" his dad called.

The little boy turned and ran toward his family. "Did you see all the colors, Daddy?" he called as he ran. "She had colors all around her!"

Evie looked at me strangely. "Do you think he..."

I looked after him as he caught up with his brothers. "Yeah, I think he was like us."

"Like you," Tristan said, holding the door open. "Not me." The bitterness in his voice bit at me.

We got off as the buzzer sounded and the doors slid closed behind us. We walked across the lobby and stood at the glass entrance doors, staring out at the night beyond.

"You ready?" Grant asked again.

I grasped at any confidence I had left before I answered and held onto it with persistence. "Let's go."

We walked out into the night air and turned, following the river on our left as we made our way to the squares, Tristan navigating on his phone. I didn't need the app on his phone to tell me where I was going, though. In fact, I was pretty sure if I closed my eyes, I would be able to follow the pressure in my chest. The locket was leading me. Leading me to its home.

We made several turns, walking through quiet streets toward Wright Square. The Spanish moss hung from tree branches, waving in the slight breeze that blew now from our backs. We crossed into the square and I heard Evie take a sharp breath in as we passed the Tomochichi monument.

"What is it?" I whispered. Before she could answer, I felt the presence of someone in front of me. A woman with long red hair stepped out of the shadows, her eyes wild with grief.

"Where is he?" she wailed, her mouth stretching into an impossible dark black hollow that took up all of her face. She began running through the square, the skirt of the long white dress she wore billowing behind her. "Where is he?"

"Did you see something?" Evie asked, twining her arm through mine.

I nodded. I could feel other spirits, pressing down on my soul. It felt like Culvers Grove. Taking a deep breath, I followed the group through the winding paths. The wailing finally faded into the distance. We turned the corner and I stopped short.

There, before me was a mammoth house. Two stories with white columns holding up the balustrade on the second floor. The windows were tall, outlined with wrought iron along the bottoms. Massive trees stood sentry in the front lawn, their limbs spreading out over the street. Along the outside, the summer grass waved in a warm breeze. A figure moved in the top window. I stared up. A woman peered at us and then disappeared, the lace curtain falling back into place.

"There's a spike here," Evie whispered.

I unwound my arm from hers and took a few steps, the locket urging me forward. My feet weren't moving on their own accord, but still, I was drawn closer. The grass gave under my shoes, a soft carpet of green. The breeze lilted my hair and I brushed a tendril from my face as I approached the front porch.

"Watch her," Evie said behind me.

I felt a hand on my elbow and glanced over to see Grant by my side.

"What are you seeing?" he asked.

"A house. Um, a huge white house." I turned my attention back to the front porch and put my foot up to step onto the first of three wide, low steps. The toe of my shoe hit something and I looked down. Nothing was there that explained why I couldn't move forward.

"Nowhere else to go," Grant whispered.

I placed my hands up and they met with something smooth and cold to the touch.

"It's an old building and you're touching the window in the front door," he said quietly.

I shook my head and looked up at the front door of the house. It was flung open and a woman stood before me. She was beautiful and familiar all at once and I took a sharp breath in. She stood at the threshold, her face expectant as she peered along the street behind us.

"Ow!" I cried out, grasping at my chest. The locket burned painfully, simultaneously pulling and pushing at the tender spot it had burrowed into my skin.

A shadow passed across the woman's face and then she was directly in front of me, her mouth stretched in a silent scream. I stumbled back as the overwhelming mixture of pain, sadness, and anger pressed against me like a physical force.

Grant steadied me and I stood straight again.

"Who do you see? Is it Charlotte?" Tristan asked from behind. His voice sounded scared.

I nodded, but never took my eyes off the woman in front of me. "Charlotte? I'm here and I brought Jacob. We need you to give Andy back."

The woman made no indication that she'd heard me. She continued to scream, the emotions sloughing off her and into the space between us.

I tried again. "Charlotte, I'm Marissa. You brought us here."

Nothing.

A moment later, I felt the warmth leave as Grant let go of my arm. It broke my concentration and the summer day fell away. We were standing on a dark street, a worn brick building in front of us. The windows were dark and the paint on the door was peeling. A FOR RENT sign perched on the dusty windowsill. I shook my head and concentrated on the past again, the pain in my chest threatening to have me black out.

"Something's wrong," I said to Evie and Tristan. "It's like she knows we're here but she can't see us."

Movement caught my eye and I looked over. Grant had moved to the larger of the two windows of the abandoned building and he stood a foot from it, his eyes transfixed on the surface.

"Grant?" I managed, before stumbling back again. My chest felt like someone had taken a hot curling iron and was rolling it across my skin. I tried to take a deep breath, but my lungs locked up with the pain and I could only manage small shallow breaths.

Grant turned, his eyes glazed over. "He's in there," he said, his voice coming out strained.

"Who?" I asked.

He stared at me, but his eyes were dark, unseeing. "Andy."

The answer was quiet, matter-of-fact. Grant turned back to the window and placed his hand up, his palm flat on the surface. Ripples spilled out from his hand and then, it disappeared into the building.

CHAPTER 15

"Grant! No!" I tried to lunge toward him, but my feet were mired in black smoke.

Black smoke!

I looked back at my friends and saw that they were trapped as well.

My gaze swung back up to Grant. He didn't look over, but continued to disappear into the window. First, his hand, then his forearm, gaining speed until his entire body was consumed by the glittering, rippling glass. A moment after he disappeared from view, the glass solidified and became a window again. A window on an abandoned building on a lonely street.

I cried out as the smoke lifted me up, tossing me around, batting at me like a cat with a new toy. It burned where it touched my skin. My cheek blistered as it swept across my face. The cries of my friends behind me rang out into the quiet night. It was playing with us. Charlotte was playing with us, entertaining herself with our anguish as the smoke threw us up into the air once more. We came down on the sidewalk across from the building. There was a nasty cracking sound as Tristan landed to my right. I landed hard on my hip. Evie lay in a heap beside me, sobs wracking her body.

I was up as soon as my feet allowed. Ignoring the pain, I ran toward the building. "Grant!" My voice cracked and I threw myself against the window again and again. I punched at it, and then looked wildly around for something to break it. My eyes fell on a crumbled piece of sidewalk near the curb and I grabbed it, stepping back to launch it at the window with all of my strength. The concrete left my fingers and arched through the air. It landed true, and I put my arms up in front of my face, prepared for the shattering of glass. Instead, the rock splintered when it came into contact with the glass, spraying me with tiny pieces of gravel and sand.

"Come on, St. Louis." Evie grabbed my arm. "We have to get out of here *now*!"

"Grant!" I screamed, tears streaming down my face.

Laughter filled my ears, spinning around me until I couldn't hear anything else. The locket knocked against my core, boring a hole inside me. I tried to center, to keep it out as Evie pulled me down the street, away from the building. Tristan followed behind, cradling his arm. We made it to the square and into the circle of light cast by a streetlamp.

I ripped my arm from Evie's grasp. "We have to go back!" I screamed. "She took Grant!"

The weight of that took me over and I raked at the locket on my chest.

"Stop taking things from me!" It came out a strangled sob as I fell to the ground. *It took my whole family, my dad, my friends, and now Grant.* A wailing built inside me and I felt the presence in the locket pressing against my chest, demanding I let it in. It took absolutely everything from me in that moment and I held onto a sliver of control, barring it with teeth gritted against the onslaught of white-hot pain. It took almost more than I had, but I finally felt the pressure subside.

I looked up at Evie. "We have to go back."

"No," she said, garnering me with a level gaze. "It, *she* will kill us." Her eyes were wary as she stared back along the street from where we had come.

A moan wound its way up from my core and I put my head in my hands. "Grant, Grant, Grant," I said his name over and over like it would bring him back to me.

"Andy's in there, too," Tristan said quietly.

His voice cut through my grief and I looked up at him. "I know."

"Time to go," Evie said under her breath.

I turned to follow her gaze and saw a wisp of black mist winding its way around the corner. Tristan held out a hand and he and Evie hauled me up, practically carrying me between them. My feet weren't working and the grief and pain mixed together, creating a ball in my middle that felt like a lead weight. Tears poured from my eyes as we wound our way through back alleys and quiet side streets toward the hotel.

Grant, Grant, Grant.

None of us spoke again until we were in the hotel room, the door locked behind us.

Tristan stood in the middle of the room, holding his arm tightly against his stomach.

"Let me look at your arm?" Evie asked as Tristan shrugged out of his coat. He winced when Evie helped him out of the left sleeve.

"What's wrong?" I asked.

"It's fine," he said.

I shook my head. I turned on all of the lights in the room and sat on the edge of the bed, my legs rubbery. "What's wrong with it?" I nodded at his arm.

Evie looked up over Tristan's arm at me. "Nothing's broken, I mean," she said looking at him, "I don't think so anyway. Your thumb's jammed, though. We need to get ice on it." She got the ice bucket and stood looking at us.

"Grant said we shouldn't go anywhere alone tonight," I mumbled. The vision of him disappearing through the glass swept over me, bringing with it a sadness that overtook my senses.

"Stay with me, St. Louis. We're going to get them back." Her eyes belied the confidence I heard in her voice.

"Fine. We'll all go get the ice."

Standing up took most of my strength and the short walk up and down the hallway depleted it completely. When we got back to the room, I locked the door again and stepped into the bathroom while Evie wrapped ice in a towel. When she left, I locked the bathroom door behind her and leaned on the counter, my head dropped to my chest where the locket still burned incessantly. A tear slipped out and splashed on the countertop.

Swinging my gaze up, I stared at my reflection in the mirror. The bags under my eyes were darker than I'd ever seen them and my cheeks were sallow and drawn in. I splashed cold water on my face and wiped away the excess with a fluffy white towel. When I brought the towel down a bit, I saw the reflection of my hands and cried out, dropping the towel.

Evie banged on the door. "St. Louis! What's wrong?"

I stared at my hands, the purple and green veins running like roadmaps along the backs of them.

"Let me in!"

I reached over and unlocked the door. Evie stepped in and I showed her my hands wordlessly.

She took a deep breath. "It's getting worse. We knew it probably would. Right?"

I nodded as she took both of my hands and led me from the bathroom like a mother leading a small child. She placed me on the bed. I sat staring at my hands, turning them over and over.

"We need to get that thing off you," Tristan said, throwing two ibuprofens in his mouth. They clicked against his teeth and set my nerves on edge again.

"You don't think I've tried?" I snapped.

"Knock it off," Evie said. She stood in the space between us. "You two have been at each other's throats since Andy was taken. Now, enough. We have to figure out what to do and you sniping at each other is not going to help."

"It hurts," I said, tears springing to my eyes. "It hurts all the time now. I don't know how long I can keep it out." A tear fell and wound its way along my cheek. I bit my lip hard and I was rewarded with the coppery taste of blood. The sharp pain gave me something else to focus on for the moment and I welcomed it.

Evie closed her eyes. She took a deep breath and opened them. "We have to figure out how to get Grant and Andy back."

"Why didn't she take the locket and Jacob tonight?" I asked. "It was like she didn't even see me. Us. She, um, she seemed to know something was there, but there was a...a..." A wave of pain clouded my vision and my thoughts got muddy.

"A barrier?" Evie offered.

I nodded. "Like the one around Culvers Grove. It was like she couldn't see through it, but she sensed something."

"It sure felt like she knew we were there," Tristan said, adjusting the ice on his thumb. "It was like she was toying with us."

"What does Charlotte want?" Evie said.

"Jacob," Tristan and I answered together.

"But, what if she doesn't just want his spirit?"

I cocked my head to the side.

"Don't do that. You look like a cocker spaniel," Evie said. She stood up and started pacing back and forth. "What if she wants you, St. Louis?"

Pain shot through my arms and I cried out.

"Stop, please?" My voice was weak and I felt exhaustion dragging me down.

"We'll take a break. You get some sleep and we'll figure some things out." Evie patted my shoulder and I moved aside so she could pull away the covers on the bed. She took my shoes off and I lay down, my head sinking into the pillow. The pillowcase was cool against my wind burned cheek and I felt my muscles contracting painfully in my legs as she covered them up.

"Keep talking," I mumbled. "Please? I don't want to feel alone."

Evie sat next to Tristan on the couch and reached out a hand to me. I slipped my hand from under the covers and took hers, allowing her to squeeze my fingers.

"It's going to be okay, St. Louis."

"How do you know?"

"Because it is. We've made it through everything that's been thrown at us. *Even* though sometimes we weren't able to save everyone," she said quickly when I started to object.

"What do we do next?" Tristan asked.

I felt so sorry for him. He sounded as scared as he had when we were in the cavern under the city, facing off with Jacob and his army.

"We have to offer Jacob in exchange for Grant and Andy. It's what she wants, but we have to figure out how to get Mattie out of the locket before that."

"Why do that?" Tristan rubbed a hand across his forehead. "If Charlotte is her mom, then won't it be a big happy family reunion?"

"Mattie's afraid of Charlotte for some reason. I think Charlotte sent the black mass I saw in the vision. It was looking for her." I tried to sit up, but only made it a few inches before the pain stopped me. I rested my head again. "If Charlotte is behind all of this, then we return Jacob to her and it stops. She and Jacob are together and it all stops."

"Do you really believe that?" Evie asked. She shoved some unruly curls behind her ear.

I pressed my lips together.

Tristan got up and started pacing the floor. "Jacob and Charlotte are in love. They get married, have a baby girl, and then Jacob leaves for some reason. He ends up in Culvers Grove and they were in love, at least for a while, according to the letter."

I turned onto my back, my muscles in spasms. "Right."

"Then, Jacob dies in Culvers Grove," Evie offered.

"And, Mattie ends up in Culvers Grove as well, hiding out as a man. She has Henry and then Henry has George and so on until we get to you." Tristan stopped for a moment, eyes raised to the ceiling and then he started pacing again. "Jacob was holed up under the town, gathering an army of souls to try to get to you, Marissa. He wasn't letting anyone leave because he knew if he could get to someone in your family line, he could get out of the town and back to Savannah. We have to get him to release the town before we return him to Charlotte. Otherwise, we've done all of this for nothing. None of us are safe."

Evie patted the cushion next to her. "Come sit. We need to rest."

Tristan grabbed the blanket from the chair and sat, spreading the blanket over his and Evie's legs. I turned over onto my side toward them, tucking my knees up against the nausea in my stomach.

"Can't we break it open?" he breathed. He stared at my chest.

I pulled the blanket up over me.

"If we break it open, then what?" Evie asked.

"Then Jacob gets out. He can go back to Charlotte."

"Martin – or Mattie – can get out and then help us get Andy and Grant."

I shook my head and tried to speak. My tongue felt like cotton and stuck to the roof of my mouth. "That's not how it works."

"How do you know?" Tristan asked. The edge was back in his voice again.

"We have to make a trade. Jacob for Andy and Grant." Sleep was pushing its way through the pain and I allowed my eyes to close for a moment. Just a moment. The pain pressed hard on me, though, and I didn't open my eyes again. I fell asleep, listening to the voices and then the movements of Evie and Tristan in the room, as they got ready for bed.

My dreams were vivid. In one, Grant was running from a pack of wolves. He kept tripping and I was watching them get closer and closer, their dripping jaws snapping at his ankles. In another, my dad was drowning in a lake of black water. I was swimming toward him, but just as I got to him, he sank below the surface, disappearing in the murky water. In the last dream, Tristan leaned over me as I slept and pressed his hand onto the locket. He cried out in pain, but kept the pressure on my chest. I turned over, trying to shelter him from the locket.

"You're part of the club now," I murmured into my pillow.

The sound of the door opening and closing a few minutes later didn't wake me up.

CHAPTER 16

"St. Louis! Wake up!"

The vestiges of my last dream fell away as I rolled over, the darkness of the room throwing me. I sat up. "What time is it?"

"Tristan's gone."

Her words sent icicles through my veins. I shoved off the covers and grabbed my phone. I texted him, staring at the screen through blurry eyes. It was late in the afternoon. We'd slept for hours.

Evie was putting on her shoes. "You know where he went."

I knew. I looked up from the screen, the hint of a dream playing around the periphery of my consciousness. I furrowed my brow, trying to grab onto it, but it slipped through my fingers like water. I stood up and moved the curtains back to allow some light into the room. An icy rain fell outside, the low clouds blocking out the light of the day. I glanced at the phone again and pulled up the maps app. The bubble with the photo of him giving two thumbs up hovered several blocks away.

"He's at Charlotte's," I said to fill the silence in the room.

"Get dressed. We have to go get him." Evie tossed my shoes to me.

I sat and put them on, the feeling of dread in my stomach growing with each movement. I stood up and caught a glimpse of myself in the mirror. The collar of my shirt had dropped below the locket. The green and purple veins raged unabated through my skin. I reached up to touch my collar, my hand brushing the locket with the motion. The dream came slamming back to me and I froze.

"He touched the locket, Evie."

She closed her eyes and took a deep breath. "We didn't have a plan, but he did. He was acting really weird after you fell asleep last night. I thought I'd calmed him down, but," her voice faded and she ran a hand over her face, her features suddenly tired and worn. She shook her head a bit and set her jaw. Standing up, she took her coat from the back of the chair. "Ready?" She looked normal again and it reminded me of the times I had watched her deal with something her mother had done. She allowed herself a moment of sadness, then changed gears, and kept pressing on.

I nodded. "Yeah."

As we headed to the elevator, Evie side-eyed me. "How are you?"

"Better than last night." I looked at my phone again, willing him to answer. "We should have gone back last night. Together."

"We couldn't. If you had lost any more strength, you wouldn't have been able to keep Charlotte out, no matter if Mattie is helping or not."

I knew she was right, but the guilt pricked at me.

When we got outside, the rain pelted us with ice. Cars passed by, but no one was out walking in this weather. Our trek to Charlotte's street was quicker than last night's and as we drew closer, the locket responded, taking up the pushing and pulling that had become so familiar at this point. I sighed and put up as many internal barriers as I could muster before following Evie through the square, our breath hanging on the frigid air.

We stood at the corner for a moment and looked at each other.

"Let me go first?" she said.

"No!" The word was out of my mouth before I had a cognizant thought.

"I have part of you in me. Maybe I can distract the black mist and let you get close enough to get Charlotte's attention. Like we did in the caves." She grabbed my hand, squeezed, and then darted around the corner.

"Evie, no!" I started around the corner and then froze.

Evie was running through the street, her feet splashing in the standing water. A tendril of black smoke appeared from the doorway of the squat brick building and followed her as she splashed down the street. She turned and smiled before disappearing around a house at the end of the block.

I gathered my strength and sped around the corner to the building. The door stood ajar a crack and I put my fingers in the space, wrapping them around the old wood and pulling. I stepped in and I was pushed back by something. I heard footsteps behind me and Evie was there. She rushed in and shoved the door closed.

"I think I lost it," she gasped, her breath hanging heavy in the cold building. Then, she turned her attention to me. "We don't have much time."

"What am I supposed to do?"

"What you do best. Go back into the past and connect with Charlotte."

I let down a barrier and the building disappeared. I was standing in the foyer of a beautiful house. A grand staircase wound up to a second floor, the banister ornate and shining. Sun streamed through the floor to ceiling windows in the sitting room to my left. A huge painting of a beautiful woman hung above the fireplace. A woman sat on the settee, her back to me. She was humming and looking down. I moved to get a better look and ran up against a barrier again.

"I can't go any further," I said to Evie.

"There's nothing in your way," was her response.

I tried again, but couldn't move. The feeling was unsettling. "It's different," I said. "This isn't like the other visions I've had of the past." I tried to take a deep breath, but the pain prevented it.

"Concentrate, St. Louis."

I used some of my energy to reach out across the space to the woman. I saw the tendrils of hair on her neck move beneath her bun, as if a small breeze had brushed against her. She stopped what she was doing and looked up. I saw her face in profile.

"It's Charlotte," I whispered.

She stood up. The front of her dress was pushed out and she placed a delicate hand on the bump as she walked to the window and peered out. A wistful look took over her features and she placed her palm flat on the glass, gazing out upon the street that ran outside the window.

"Jacob, my love," she whispered. "Come back to us."

The locket twisted on my chest, pulling the skin and I cried out, the vision fading away.

"What happened?" Evie asked. She had her hands on my arms, ready if I fell.

I shook my head. "She was pregnant and she was looking for Jacob."

"Can she hear you?"

"I don't know."

Evie looked behind her at the doorway and her eyes widened. I followed her gaze and took a step back. Black smoke pressed against the windows, blocking the view. It undulated and swirled with sinister intent.

"How are we going to get out of here?" I squeaked.

Evie shook her head and took a deep breath. "First, try to get to Charlotte. Then, we'll worry about getting out of here."

I nodded and turned my attention back to the building interior. Pressing my lips together, I tried to delve into the past again. The building fell away and the house reappeared. This time, though, it was as if I was viewing it through a gritty film. The colors of the parlor were muted and a storm raged outside the windows. Charlotte was there again and she walked toward the fire roaring in the fireplace. The painting above the mantle had changed. I squinted. The face of the woman wasn't quite in focus, but this time, I realized that the painting was of Charlotte. *Was that different?* When she turned, I saw that she was no longer pregnant. She held a letter in her hands. A baby was crying in the basinet by the window and Charlotte turned her head toward the sound. The movement was jerky and off center. She looked back down at the letter and a screeching cry escaped her lips. She ripped it to shreds and tossed the paper into the fire. The shreds caught and burned hot.

The baby cried again and Charlotte moved toward the basinet, her left side moving out of sync with her right. She peered into the cradle, her head tilted. A strange smile twisted her features as she lifted the newborn baby. She brought it to her bosom and looked out the window.

She spoke, her voice like layers of many voices speaking together as one. "Your father has left us, little one. He has found love on his travels and she has taken him away from us." She looked down, regarding the baby with hatred in her eyes.

My stomach twisted as I watched.

Charlotte turned, moving across the room with the baby in her arms. She opened a small trinket box and lifted something out. It caught the light of the fire and glinted.

"Let's send your father a gift. Something to remember me by."

I gasped. It was the locket.

Charlotte stopped and looked up at me. Her eyes were black caverns. She tilted her head and stared at me. I took a step away from her and felt Evie at my back.

"What's wrong?"

"She sees me," I breathed.

In a flash, Charlotte was standing before me. Her head was lowered and she peered at me through hooded black eyes. A smiled drew up one side of her mouth. "Hello, Marisssaaaaa."

Tears sprang to my eyes and I felt my insides loosen. My chest rose and fell as I stared at her.

"I want my friends back," I said, my voice shaking.

She jerked her chin toward the mirror on the wall behind her. I looked past her and saw Andy, Grant, and Tristan. They were lying amid a garden near a fountain, their bodies twisted like Sam's had been at the bottom of the well. Black smoke whirled around them and they were moaning in pain. Grant turned his head toward me. His eyes were wide and blood trickled from them. I cried out and pressed against the film between us.

Laughter reached my ears and filled my consciousness. Charlotte considered me from her black eyes. "You have something I want." Her voice wound around me, filling my senses with an oily slick feeling of dread.

"He loved you, you know," I said. "Jacob. He loved you and died loving you. There was never anyone else."

Charlotte's features grew strange. It was like hiccup in the glamour. Her face split into two. One, familiar and filled with sadness; one, unfamiliar, beautiful, but dark and twisted. Then she snapped back together.

"We want our friends back." This time, my voice was strong.

Charlotte's face twitched and she brought her hand out toward me. "And you know what you have to give in exchange."

Let me in.

In that moment, I knew. I knew that Jacob wasn't the only thing she wanted. She wanted me. Just like Evie said. Different city, different characters, but the same ending. I was going to have to give up myself in order to save my friends and family. The sinking feeling that came with that realization almost broke me. Charlotte stared at me while tears burned my eyes.

Give me what I want.

Her hand pressed against the film, then broke through. On this side, her hand was gnarled and twisted, the blood-red fingernails like daggers.

Evie drew in a sharp breath behind me and pulled. "No, that's not Charlotte!"

I whirled around and stopped short. At the windows, the black smoke was thick, beating like a heartbeat as it waited to envelop us.

"We can't get out!" I shouted.

A sonic boom erupted behind us. I felt it inside me and all around. My ears rang. I cried out and turned to look behind me. The house had disappeared and the empty building remained. Dust filtered from the rafters. Charlotte was gone. A hag stood in her place, her hand outstretched, long stringy gray hair hanging in her face. Her eyes peered out at me, drawing me into their blackness. The locket burned and pulled away from my skin. Blood poured from the wound, warm on my chest.

"Evie!" I screamed.

"I see her," Evie's voice caught. She looked back at the smoke at the door. Her movements were furtive, indecisive. Like a trapped animal.

The hag moved toward me, the locket pulling from my skin with persistence. Tears ran down my face. Hopelessness filled me. This was it. Evie wrapped her arms around me and we faced the approaching danger.

"It appears as if you ladies may need some assistance."

Evie and I spun around. There, in the doorway was an old man, stooped with age. His eyes were kind and he leaned upon an ivory cane. The smoke arched away from him, creating a tunnel. Rain fell in sheets onto the street beyond.

He held his hand out and smiled. "Come with me, child."

CHAPTER 17

Evie stared at me open-mouthed for a moment and then yanked hard on my arm, toward the man at the door. At our backs, the hag shrieked, the sound filling every corner of the building. My vision wavered but I felt Evie's grasp on my hand and concentrated on it. The locket burned. Blood pulsed in my veins. The skin on my chest screamed with pain.

As we got nearer to the man, the pressure on my chest lessened and I could breathe again. I turned to look back at the woman. Her mouth was stretched in a scream, and as we followed the old man through the archway of smoke, she screamed again. The glass in the windows shattered, sending shards of glass skittering across the wet pavement as we emerged from the smoke tunnel into the street on the other side. The door slammed shut behind us and the windows were intact again. The old building sat, innocuous, in the late afternoon storm.

He led us through the rainy streets. Evie and I leaned on each other, the wind lashing the icy rain in our faces as we walked.

He turned to look at us. "Just a short way now."

A church rose ahead, the steeple reaching up into the low clouds. The steps led from the front door to the sidewalk lined by neatly trimmed hedges. He waved us around the corner and we followed him toward a small building made of stone that sat near the back of the church. He stood at the door and pressed his hand against it. It opened and he stepped inside. Evie stood a few feet away, her eyes watchful.

The old man appeared at the door again. "Come in, now. Get warm."

I glanced over at Evie. "Should we?"

"Should we what?"

"He said we should come in and get warm."

"This one's a ghost, St. Louis. I can't see him when we break our connection." A smile broke across Evie's features. "But, if he has somewhere for us to get warm, I'm all for it." She ducked into the door and entered the small building.

I followed. The small room was crowded with machinery and paint cans. I looked around for a place to sit and he closed the door behind us. He turned and held up his hands. As he did, the room expanded, filling with a large table, chairs, and a large antique stove. A fireplace appeared on the far wall as it pushed back and a fire sprang up within, instantly warming the room around us.

"Can you see this?" I said out of the corner of my mouth.

She shook her head. "I can feel it, though. It's warmer, right?"

The old man stepped over and placed a pale wrinkled hand on Evie's shoulder.

She gasped and looked around. "I can see it," she whispered. "And I can see *him*."

He smiled and patted her shoulder. "Have a seat."

A pair of plush chairs appeared near the fireplace, worn leather with fluffy blankets draped across their backs. The old man indicated a chair for Evie and I told her to sit. She shrugged out of her wet coat and placed it on the hearth to dry. Then she sat gingerly in a chair, wrapping one of the blankets around her.

"You sit here," he said, waving his hand. A chair pulled out from the table and I sat, draping my coat across the back of the chair next to it. He bent and looked at my chest. "We will get this fixed up before we talk." He turned and stood at the stove, a large copper pot appearing before him on the burner. The house was filled with the scent of the herbs he took from a string above the stove where they hung drying. The mixture in the pot bubbled pleasantly and I let the warmth overtake me for a moment.

He brought a clay bowl over and pulled a chair out. He sat facing me, his wise eyes considering me. I got the feeling he was sizing me up. The wrinkles around his eyes deepened as he smiled. He nodded at my chest and I moved my shirt collar down a bit.

Concern took over his eyes and he clucked his tongue. "Powerful black magic," he murmured as he washed the area with a white rag dipped in warm water. The first few times he brought the towel away from my chest, it was stained pink and my blood swirled in the basin as he swished the towel in the water and then wrung it out. I gritted my teeth against the pain. It wasn't as sharp as the burning before, but the ragged skin around the locket was tender. After cleaning it, he used a piece of cloth to spread the pungent salve from the clay bowl onto my skin. The second it touched my skin, relief spread through me. The burning was cooled and I took the first deep breath I'd taken since putting the locket around my neck in Culvers Grove. My lungs filled with delicious air and I relished the feeling of ease that spread through my core. I concentrated on my breathing. In and out, air rushing in and swirling in my lungs.

I allowed a smile to part my lips. "Thank you."

He nodded and waved his hand. The clay bowl and basin of pink water disappeared. "Let us speak now. I am sure you have many questions." He stood up and used his cane to walk over to a rocking chair that appeared across from the leather chair.

I slipped under a blanket in the chair next to Evie. "Are you good?" I asked.

She nodded. "Is it weird that at this point in our friendship I'm not even questioning this?"

The old man regarded us, his hands folded on the top of his cane as he rocked slowly.

"I don't mean to be rude, but who are you?" I blurted out. "Where did you come from? How were you able to save us from that, that, *thing*? What was that? That wasn't Charlotte, was it?"

He smiled at me. "That was Charlotte, and it was not. To explain, though, we must go back many, many years. Back to when I was a couturier."

Evie looked over at me and raised an eyebrow. I shook my head slowly.

He began to speak. "My name is Christopher Williams. I met Otto Adams when I was a dressmaker in England and we became fast friends. My wife, Harriet, and I were nearly part of the family and treated their daughter like one of our own. When Otto's beloved wife succumbed to typhoid fever, he became a broken man. Wanting to leave behind the sadness that her death brought, he made plans to sail to the Americas. He talked us into going, and in the autumn of 1792, Otto, Harriet, myself, and Otto's daughter – his sweet little Lottie, he called her – arrived in Savannah."

"Charlotte," I whispered to Evie.

"His business in the states was imports and exports, and business was very good. Mine, however, was not so lucrative, and Harriet threatened to sail back to her family in England unless I made more money. I found a way," his face darkened a moment, "and it is what led to the greatest regret of my life. And my death."

Mr. Williams sat back in his chair and closed his eyes. I could see his throat working as he struggled. Finally, he sat back up and regarded us with cloudy eyes. "I purchased a journal from a tinker. He told me that it contained a multitude of spells, enchantments, and root working from the conjurers – it has been called many things through the years, but most know it now as Hoodoo."

I glanced over at Evie.

"I used the journal to make potions and tinctures that people bought for a handsome sum. I thought that the spells in the journal were little more than a list of ingredients and was a bit upset that I had been so foolish, but I was preying on the foolishness of others, so what place did I have to complain? It wasn't until the summer of 1806 that I realized the full danger of what was contained within that journal. I remember that it was a sweltering year and Lottie came to my shop, needing a new dress commissioned for a garden party. With her father's good fortune, she had grown to be an insufferable child, eighteen, but without any of the empathy or social good graces that customarily accompanied a young woman of her age. That day, I had been careless and left the door open to the room that held my potions. When Lottie found them, I showed her the journal and admitted everything. I asked her to keep this from her father, as I did now want him to know of my shameful business dealings. After we met about the dress, I returned to the room to discover that the journal was gone."

"Lottie took it?"

Mr. Williams nodded slowly. "Yes, child, Lottie took it. And, what she did with it was nothing short of evil."

The locket twitched on my chest, but didn't hurt. I ignored the movement.

"Did you try to get it back?" Evie asked.

He nodded again. "I asked her about it when she came in for a fitting the next week. She smiled sweetly and pulled it from her reticule. She made up some apology for accidentally taking it and handed it over to me."

"I'll bet she'd already written everything down to keep," Evie said.

"You're young, but already smarter than I was." Mr. Williams shifted his weight, his chair creaking. His voice had an edge to it and I could feel waves of guilt washing off of him. "Lottie used the information contained within that journal to begin to create darkness. I began to study the original with fervor, hoping for a way to offset her growth, but I was not nearly as adept as her, though, and I watched as she grew stronger at bending the will of those around her through curses."

"Curses?" I breathed.

Mr. Williams' eyes flitted to my chest. "Yes, child. And you are wearing an object that was the recipient of one of her worst."

We sat in silence.

Finally, I cleared my throat. "Charlotte was awful."

Mr. Williams glanced up. His eyes were watery. "No, no, child. Charlotte was the kindest soul I ever had the pleasure to meet. It was her cousin, Ottolie – Lottie – that was the dark one."

CHAPTER 18

"I don't understand. I saw Charlotte in the locket. *She* was helping Jacob take souls."

Mr. Williams smiled slowly, sadly. He leaned over his cane and stared directly into my eyes. "I want to show you something. Much more will become clear." He sat back in the rocker and closed his eyes. He mumbled something under his breath and a small rectangle appeared in his hands. He turned it toward us and I could see that it was a mirror. The surface was dark and reflected my face. Evie adjusted her blanket and moved up in the cushion for a better look.

Our images began to swirl and move. I squinted as something came into focus. It was Charlotte's house. A carriage was stopped in the street in front of the house and the door was ajar. A man offered his hand and Charlotte stepped out, clad in a beautiful yellow dress with ivory buttons on the bodice.

She smiled. "Thank you, Father."

Mr. Williams' voice spoke to us from the room. "Charlotte's father, Louis, was Otto's brother. He and his wife came to Savannah several years before Otto, attempting to find their fortune in the Americas. Unfortunately, Louis did not have the business sense his brother possessed and he and his wife fell on hard times. They both became ill and passed away in the month after this garden party."

"Charlotte, my sweet cousin!"

The squeal brought our attention back to the mirror and we watched as a beautiful young woman ran up to Charlotte and embraced her. The young woman had dark hair drawn up in an intricate updo. She wore a gorgeous pink lace dress that was head and shoulders above the dresses around her at the garden party.

"Ottolie?" I asked and looked up at Mr. Williams.

He nodded his head once, curtly. "Lottie Adams."

Lottie leaned into Charlotte and whispered something in her ear. Charlotte's smile faded a bit and she looked down at her dress and attempted to smooth out the material that had wrinkled in the heat during the ride. Lottie whirled around and walked back toward the middle of the garden, leaving Charlotte standing alone on the veranda.

Near the fountain, a man stood talking to a small group of people, his foot propped up on the stone edge of the fountain and a glass in his hand. He smiled and I drew in a breath.

"It's Jacob!" I exclaimed. He looked so much different from the man I saw in the vision and the entity of rage I saw in the cavern, but I was sure it was him. He reminded me of Sam a little.

Evie moved closer to me, her shoulder brushing mine. "He has Sam's eyes."

Lottie marched right into the middle of the group and smiled up at Jacob. He smiled at her but then looked up and saw Charlotte standing at the doors. He stared for a moment and then blinked. Leaning in, he asked Lottie something and gestured to Charlotte with his glass. Lottie rolled her eyes a bit and her mouth pinched as she said something back to him. Jacob said something to her and then walked toward Charlotte, grabbing a glass of tea from a table on his way.

"Charlotte Adams?" he asked, handing her the glass. His voice wrapped around her name and his eyes studied her face.

Charlotte smiled, the color rising in her cheeks. "Thank you, sir."

Jacob threw his head back and laughed. "My name is Jacob. Jacob Smith to be more precise. And, I am not a 'sir', though my father would be pleased with the presumption of my stature."

They spoke to one another for several minutes and I found myself smiling. It was like watching the beginning of a romance movie.

"They're perfect for each other," I said.

The feeling of warmth and light enveloped them as they wandered to the back of the garden and sat on a bench swing, talking and laughing. The mirror's image swung back to Lottie, standing by the fountain. She was watching the couple, her head lowered and shoulders drawn up. It felt like the same look Charlotte had when I saw her vision in the building. It was unsettling and I brought an absent hand to my chest. There were several more glimpses of the garden party, and in each of them, Jacob and Charlotte were inseparable. Talking, laughing, and dancing. Falling in love.

Suddenly, the image faded and then we were in a hallway. An open door stood to our right. Through it, several men's voices could be heard.

"If his heart is set on this mission, then I beseech you, Bishop Andrew, to send him somewhere safe."

A chuckle. "By nature of the life of a circuit rider, there is some understood danger, Otto. Surely, you know that."

"I understand the nature of this occupation, but he shared with my Lottie that he is adamant that he be allowed to spread the Word to those who would otherwise not have access to it. It is his life's work and he wants to leave as soon as possible after the wedding."

"There is talk that the tribes have moved on from the territories in Missouri. We could send him there."

"How long would he be gone?"

"Most circuits last two years, but we could make an exception should it be deemed necessary. Should he leave this fall, he could begin his circuit before the winter's hardships."

The image faded and we were back in the garden. Everything was decorated, summer flowers everywhere. People stood in the garden, facing a beautiful arbor hung with flowering ivy. A pastor stood under the arbor, flanked by Jacob and another man on one side and Lottie on the other, resplendent in a dress the color of hyacinth. Charlotte and Otto passed by. Charlotte was in white and the smile on her face was unwavering.

The wedding was beautiful and Charlotte and Jacob looked happier than I could have imagined. The scene changed then and it was early fall. Jacob was packing up the saddlebags on his horse on the street outside the Adams' house. Charlotte descended the porch steps and handed him a knit scarf.

Mr. Williams cleared his throat, startling me. "Otto insisted that since her parents had passed, Charlotte move into his home during Jacob's absence."

"I made this for you, my husband, so that you can stay warm on your travels." Her voice hitched a bit and she fought back tears.

Jacob reached down and caressed her face with a gentle hand. "I will be gone but a short time and then I shall return to you." His hand moved to rest on her stomach. "To you *both*."

Charlotte leaned into him. "I do not want you to go," she whispered.

He kissed the top of her head. "I do not want to leave. However, it has been decreed by the church and I must."

The front door whipped open and Lottie ran from inside. "Jacob!" she cried, rushing down the steps. Her cheeks were red and her eyes looked as if she had been crying. When she reached him, she held out a small package wrapped in cloth and tied with twine. "It's a gift. A wedding present. I am sorry it was not finished in time for the ceremony, but you must take this with you." Her eyes never left Jacob's face as he smiled and took the package from her.

"Thank you, Miss Adams."

Charlotte took a step back and wrapped her arms around herself. It was a familiar gesture; one I had used when I felt like my pieces were falling apart. I wondered if she knew this would be the last time she would see Jacob? I thought of Grant. *What was the last thing I'd said to him?* Panic overtook me. I couldn't remember. But this was different, right? I would see Grant again.

"It is beautiful," Jacob said, holding up the locket by the chain. It turned, glinting ominously in the bright sun.

"Open it," Lottie said, dipping her head and peering out at him from under her lashes.

Charlotte seemed not to notice Lottie's flirting, but stood instead staring at Jacob, as if she was trying to memorize his face.

Jacob pried apart the locket and stared inside. He looked up at Charlotte and smiled, and then turned the locket in her direction. "I will be able to see your face, now, anytime I wish," he whispered and drew her close, kissing her.

Lottie's lips were moving as she watched the couple and her eyes glazed over, turning almost black within their sockets. She smiled; her teeth bared. Then, she shook her head and seemed to gain her composure again.

"Thank you for this," Jacob said to Lottie. He swept the chain over his neck and dropped the locket into his shirt collar, then turned to Charlotte again. "I shall wear you next to my heart, my love."

They embraced and the image faded.

"She never saw him again," I whispered.

"No, child, she never did."

I cleared my throat and peered into the mirror as the image shifted. This time, Charlotte was in the parlor. The painting above the mantel smiled at her.

"Is that Lottie? In the painting?"

Mr. Williams shook his head. "It's her mother."

Charlotte was sitting on the settee, her back to me. A breeze passed along her neck and she looked up.

"This is what I saw in the building!" I cried. "I saw this, Evie!"

Charlotte stood up then, her stomach pushing against the bodice of her dress. She walked over to the window and placed her palm on the windowpane.

"Jacob, my love," she whispered. "Come back to us."

I mouthed the words along with her.

The image changed again and it was the next vision I'd seen in the building. This time, though, the film was gone and the colors were bright and happy. The painting above the mantle was of Lottie's mother, not Charlotte. I furrowed my brow as Charlotte stood, holding a letter in her hands. She smiled at it, and covered her mouth with a dainty hand, her eyes gleaming with tears. A baby cried in the basinet near the window and Charlotte looked up. Her features softened and she cooed as she walked over to the cradle, folding the letter and placing it in the pocket that hung at her side.

"Sweet baby Mattie," she cooed at the baby as she gently lifted her from the cradle.

"This isn't right," I said. "It's not like before…"

"That's because your vision was being manipulated. *She* wanted you to see something else."

Mr. Williams' words shot ice through my veins. I thought back to Evie's time in the cavern. What she had seen. What Sam and my dad had been forced to see. Was Lottie behind it all? Had she cursed the locket so that she could cause pain to everyone who came into contact with it?

Charlotte held the baby, rocking slowly back and forth, as she stared out the window. "Your father is coming back soon, little one. We will be a family again." Her voice held such love and hope in it that it brought tears to my eyes.

A movement near the back wall caught my eye and I looked into the shadow in the corner. Standing there was Lottie. Her hair hung, unkempt and stringy, over a stained dress. She rocked back and forth slowly, mimicking Charlotte's motion. The way she stared at Charlotte and the baby sent dread into my core.

Another shift and we were running through a forest with Charlotte.

"Where is she, Mr. Williams?" Charlotte cried.

"Up ahead. Just up ahead."

The path ran along a small creek for a bit and then dropped into a valley. The underbrush grew thick here and Charlotte's dress snagged on the bramble as she ran. Animals rushed through the forest around them and a crow cawed in the gathering darkness. A pinprick of light in the distance appeared as they ran.

"There!" Mr. Williams said. They ran until they came upon a large tree, older than anything around it in the forest, its branches gnarled and covered in Spanish moss. A small cabin was built into the side of the tree, blending in with the forest around it. Mr.

Williams and Charlotte ran up to the window and peered in. The cabin had a dirt floor. Shelves cut into the mortar had been fashioned along the walls and were lined with jars and clay pots. Herbs hung from the ceiling and a chicken squawked from a cage hanging near the door. Candles were lit and a small fire was crackling in the fireplace, a basin of water placed near it.

"I don't see her," Charlotte whispered.

"She's in there," Mr. Williams said. His voice sounded scared.

Movement from the back of the cabin. Lottie, her hair nearly hiding her face, stepped from the darkness. Her dress was ragged and torn and her feet were bare beneath. She shuffled to the basin, holding a bundle tightly to her chest. Then, the bundle in her arms shifted and began crying.

"Mattie!" Charlotte cried out.

Lottie's head snapped up and she looked at us with black eyes. A smile parted her lips and her teeth were sharp. She tilted her head a bit and unwrapped the small child. Muttering to herself, she held the child above the basin.

Charlotte screamed and ran to the door, banging upon it with her fists. Mr. Williams followed as a splash sounded from the window. The vision got shaky as Mr. Williams turned, looking for something to take down the door. Charlotte's screams filled the night as she beat upon the door. His eyes fell on an axe lying near some chopped wood and he ran over, grabbing the axe from the stump.

"Move!" he demanded and Charlotte turned, her eyes wild.

His breath came hard as he swung the axe, bringing it down against the door over and over again. The wood began to splinter and the orange glow from the fire showed through. He swung once more and the door shattered. Charlotte ran in.

Lottie raised her hands toward Charlotte.

"No!" she shouted, sending out electricity from her hands. It arced and then settled into Charlotte's chest, throwing her back where she lay still on the threshold.

Mr. Williams ran in and grabbed the child from the basin of water. She was rigid and her lips were blue. He held a hand up to Lottie, creating a barrier. Lottie growled like a wounded animal. She paced along the border, murmuring something under her breath, her head swinging back and forth, her eyes black. He backed out of the cabin, tapping Charlotte with the toe of his boot as he passed.

Her eyes fluttered open and settled on him. "Hello, Mr. Williams. When is Jacob coming home?"

"Come now," he said, backing away.

Charlotte stood and followed him as they made their way back through the forest. When they got a distance away from the cabin, he turned and ran, holding the child against him and pulling Charlotte along. They ran back to Charlotte's house. When they got to the kitchen, they burst through the door and he lay the child on the table. Mr. Williams shut the door and placed Charlotte in a chair. He stood looking down at Mattie. Her dripping brown locks were spread around her in a halo and her eyes were closed. The image wavered through his tears.

A mist of color hovered above her, reds and yellows sparking within the swirling white cloud. He gathered his energy and it flowed through him, blue electricity filled with warmth, and then he placed his hands on Mattie's heart. The energy flowed through her, searching for something. Then, it moved through her fingertips and stopped, almost like a snake poised to strike. Colors reached out from the mist and met with the blue electricity. It twined together, and the blue electricity grabbed hold of the mist, turning it rainbow colors that moved with an ethereal glow. The electricity coaxed the mist forward, back toward the little girl. Then, the mist shot into Mattie and the electricity returned to Mr. Williams with a sonic boom. He stumbled back and bent over, breathing hard.

"Mama?"

Mr. Williams looked up and Mattie sat on the table, her cheeks rosy and her eyes bright.

"Oh, sweet child," he cried, emotion making his voice almost a croak.

"What is going on in here?" Otto strode in, his boots heavy on the floor.

"Mattie was too close to the creek, Father. She fell in and I saved her."

Mr. Williams turned.

Lottie stood at the door, her hair swept up into a neat bun and her dress immaculate.

Otto gathered Mattie in his arms. "Let's get you into some dry clothes, eh? You've had quite the adventure tonight, haven't you?"

"I told her she shouldn't play there, but you know how little girls are." Lottie cast a warning glance in Mr. Williams' direction as she followed her father into the house.

The mirror darkened for a moment. I leaned back, my heart racing. I looked over at Evie and she sat, staring at the mirror, her mouth open.

"I don't know what to say," I said after a long silence. "That was awful."

Mr. Williams nodded. "After that, Mattie was changed."

"She had colors around her," Evie said. "Did you see that?"

I nodded my head.

"Like you, St. Louis. She looked just like you."

"Mattie began to see things that weren't there. *People* that weren't there," Mr. Williams said. He took a long drink of coffee from a steaming cup that appeared next to him.

"She almost died," Evie said. "She had one foot in this world and one in the other. Guess we know where your family's superpowers originated from, huh?"

I considered her for a moment then nodded my head. "Mr. Williams, what happened to Charlotte?"

He peered over his cup and regarded me. Then, taking a deep breath, he spoke softly. "Charlotte was never the same. She wandered around the house, asking when Jacob was coming home, even after so much time had passed that we knew he was never to return to Savannah."

CHAPTER 19

"Jacob died in Culvers Grove," I said quietly. "He was sick and died. Then, the locket pulled his spirit into it. He's been there, holding the souls from leaving since he died."

"Not him, child."

I looked up at the old man's cloudy eyes. "It was Lottie? Why?"

"There is binding magic that is governed by the dark arts. In Hoodoo, a spirit can be contained in a jar with a candle burning on top. Like a lightning bug. I believe that Lottie twisted this so that Jacob could never return to Charlotte. If she could keep him in Missouri, trapped, he could never come home."

"So, *she's* creating the barrier," Evie breathed.

"Why over the entire town, though? Why not over just Jacob?"

"She must have known the area Mattie was in, and if she cast the net wide enough..." Evie stared at me. "This is so big, St. Louis."

I nodded. "I know, but why does she want Jacob now, after all this time?"

Mr. Williams shook his head. "I do not believe that it is only Jacob that she wants anymore."

His words floated around me in the room, beating against my head. I took a deep breath.

"She wants me."

"Before, she only wanted to keep Jacob *from* Charlotte. To cause them the pain she felt when Jacob rejected her. What she wants now, what she has wanted for years and years is something very different. Much more important to her. Do you wonder why your friend could see her but not me back in the building?"

"You could see him, because you were touching me. Like Sam and Melanie, right?" I looked at Evie.

"But when I wasn't touching you, I couldn't see him until, well, until he did whatever this is," she swung a hand around her. "But I wasn't touching you when I saw her, St. Louis. She was as real as you and me."

I swallowed. "She's not a spirit, is she? She's *real*? But how? It's been..."

"Over two hundred years," he finished for me. "To exist, she has summoned the darkest magic. She has been using bodies no longer encumbered with spirits. Empty vessels."

His words sunk in and I felt gooseflesh rise along my arms. "Lottie wants me because I can walk between the worlds." I swallowed. "If she has me..."

"She can live forever," Evie whispered.

Mr. Williams nodded. "But it was not you that she wanted first. For many years, I stayed near to protect Mattie, and to a lesser degree, Charlotte. Charlotte died when Mattie turned sixteen and her spirit set up residence in the parlor, forever waiting for Jacob's return. That year was when I got sick with the yellow fever. I knew I would no longer be able to offer protection."

The mirror glimmered and I sat up, focusing on the vision it was bringing forth.

Mattie stood before us, her hair cut short and a pair of trousers and a white shirt gleaming in the summer sun. They were standing near the docks, people bustling around them.

"You understand what you must do?" Mr. Williams' voice was hoarse in the vision and he bent, overtaken by a coughing fit.

Mattie's brow furrowed. "Who will take care of you if I am gone?"

He waved a hand in her direction. "I will be fine. You go to the stagecoach and tell them that you are bound for St. Joseph, Missouri."

"The pony express," she said quietly, then dropped her voice even more. "Won't she find me?"

"She will be looking for our sweet Mattie," Mr. Williams said, his voice breaking. "She will not be looking for a strapping young man bound for adventure in the west."

She smiled and turned to look back at the stagecoach. The driver motioned to her, "Are you Martin Smith?"

Mattie nodded. "One minute, please."

Mr. Williams' tone turned serious. "I will keep her tempered as best I can for as long as I can. You go. Be safe and remember never to let your guard down. The second you do; she will find you."

Mattie nodded, her eyes filling with tears as she grabbed both of his hands in her own. "Thank you for everything, Mr. Williams. Your kindness to my family and me will never be forgotten."

She turned and ran toward the stagecoach. The image wavered and then disappeared as the coach drove away, wheels bouncing along the ballasts.

Mr. Williams swept his hand and the mirror disappeared. He sat back in the chair. His eyes were raised toward the ceiling and he was breathing hard. A tear slipped from his eye and wound its way through the deep wrinkles along his cheek before dropping onto his collar. A dark ring spread.

I sat, letting everything I'd learned swim around in my head. Finally, I spoke. "If Lottie couldn't find Mattie, then why did she wait until I came along? Why didn't she try to take Henry or George? Why not my grandma or my dad? Why me?" My voice amped up a notch with each name. Then quieter, "Why me?"

"When she was strong, in a new vessel, Lottie would send out monsters, black things made of smoke and death to search for Mattie. Most of the time, she did not find anything, but on a search almost two hundred years ago now, a monster reported a girl from another time in a cabin on the outskirts of Jacob's town. A girl with a locket around her neck. She knew then that the line had been continued, and that Mattie had passed her gift down to a descendant."

I shot a look over at Evie. Her eyes were wide.

Mr. Williams continued. "Lottie did not know how Mattie and the girl were connected; only that they were and that she had to wait."

"Wait for me to come to Savannah looking for her," I said wryly.

"Right, but for two hundred years?" Evie asked.

Mr. Williams looked over at her. "Love is patient, but hate is unending. If it roots in, it never goes away. It stays there, festering inside a person, twisting their insides until they become something unrecognizable."

I touched the locket around my neck and then looked up at him. "How do we stop her?"

"While my powers have faded as I grow distant from my living self, she has grown more powerful the more years that passed. I was unable to stop her then, but am little more than an inconvenience for her now." He shook his head. "I do not know how to stop her."

I could feel his guilt hanging heavily in the air around us. No one said anything for a long time, and then Evie spoke.

"You've been here since the 1800s, Mr. Williams. You've given up seeing your wife again so that you could keep Mattie safe."

He brought his head down and looked at her. "It was my duty. I helped to create that evil. It was only fair that I kept watch over what I created."

"No, you were tricked into sharing information. After that, she did with it what she wanted. You didn't create that *thing* we saw in the abandoned building. You shouldn't feel any guilt."

He smiled a sad smile. "Without guilt, what do I have?"

"You have an excuse to move on," I said quietly. "You've done more than enough, Mr. Williams. You promised to watch out for Mattie and protect her. You've done that now in her life and her death."

"I don't know how to move on now, even if I could," he said.

"Let us try to help you?" I asked. I pressed out, feeling for spirits that were hiding in the periphery. I found something and sent out a tendril of emotion. *He's here. He's ready, now.*

"It's kind of our thing. But, before you go, do you know where she keeps the spirits she takes?"

I looked over at Evie and raised my eyebrow. "What are you thinking?"

She shook her head once, almost imperceptibly, and leaned in to listen to Mr. Williams.

"Her cabin," he said. "She hides it with powerful dark magic, though. Only those like me can see it."

"You mean, ghosts? St. Louis can see it, then. Where is it?" Evie sat up on the edge of the chair, her cheeks red.

He regarded us for a moment and then waved a hand. A vision of a cabin appeared, almost hidden among the gnarled roots of a gigantic tree.

"Travel west along the river to the canal. Go through the forest until you meet the railroad tracks. Turn three times to the left and three times to the right and the Tree of the Dead will appear for you. You will find the spirits in a cabin at its base."

"Thank you," I said. I felt a presence behind me. "Now, it's time for you to go, isn't it?"

Mr. Williams looked up at me, but then his line of vision skimmed over my head.

"Harriet," he breathed and stood up.

I turned to look behind me. A woman emerged from the wall, her eyes never leaving Mr. Williams' face. They met near the table and he reached out to hold her hands. When they touched, his shoulders slumped in a silent sob.

Harriet touched his cheek. "Come now, sweet husband, it is time for us to be together."

Joy enveloped them in a white light, gathering them together in an embrace. The light shot up through the ceiling. As it did, the room returned to its original form. Evie looked over at me and raised an eyebrow. We grabbed our coats and got up from the paint cans we were sitting on and dashed outside. The light spread along the sky, arcing out from the center into the darkening rainclouds. Slowly, the white light dissipated, and then turned into lightning flashes as thunder rolled.

"What now?" Evie asked.

"We go take down Lottie."

CHAPTER 20

"Where do you think she's keeping them?" Evie ran to catch up with me. She grabbed my arm and turned me toward her. "St. Louis, if she's trapped Andy, Tristan, and Grant, then where do you think she's keeping them?"

"I-I saw them in the garden," I said, "at Charlotte's house. They were twisted and moaning." I took a hitching breath. "You didn't see them, Evie," I whispered. My heart cramped as I thought of Grant turning toward me, his eyes pleading for help. I would do anything to get that image out of my mind.

Evie pulled me over to a bench that sat in the shelter of a large tree. The limbs broke the rain a bit. The iron slats were cold on my legs and I shivered.

"Think about it. Lottie wouldn't keep them in the building where someone might hear them." She shook her head.

"I saw them! They were there!"

"You saw them, but was it what Lottie wanted you to see? Think back, St. Louis. What was really there?"

I hated doing it with every fiber of my being, but I thought back to what I saw in the vision. They were moaning, twisted, bleeding, but there was something else. I squeezed my eyes and pulled away the layer. Underneath, was a vision of their bodies, still and quiet, lying on the floor of the abandoned building.

Evie's voice was quiet, thoughtful. "She would have incapacitated them; left them unable to call out for help."

"She took their spirits from their bodies?" I asked. I opened my eyes and let the thought settle for a moment. "She wouldn't have done that. W-when we give Jacob to her, she has to be able to give us back our friends, not just their bodies, right?"

Evie stared at me.

A sick feeling boiled in my stomach, rolling around and growing bigger. "She wasn't planning on giving them back, was she?"

Evie sat down next to me. "I don't think so. I don't think that was ever the plan."

"Then, what was she going to do with the bodies?" I asked. "Never mind. Three teens found dead in a building in Savannah."

We sat in silence for a bit, watching the rain stream through the halos created by the streetlights turning on along the squares. People were returning home from work, blissfully unaware of the battle for life and death going on in the city they called home. It would be completely dark soon. We needed to get going.

I sighed. "If their spirits are in the cabin, and their bodies are at the building, then we need to get their spirits first."

"There she is," Evie said, bumping against me with her shoulder.

"Then we find Lottie and we offer her Jacob and Mattie for our friends." I worked hard to keep my true thoughts from showing in my aura. If it came down to it, I was willing to give myself to stop everyone from hurting. I was willing to give Lottie what she wanted. I would let her in.

Evie tilted her head. "We can't do that to Mattie and Jacob. They don't deserve it."

I cleared my throat and tried to exude confidence. "It won't be permanent."

Evie squinted at me.

"Once we have them all back, we'll be powerful enough to stop her." *No, we won't.*

"How?"

I shook my head. "I don't know quite yet, but we'll cross that bridge when we get there." Tears threatened and I blinked rapidly.

"That bridge sounds awful," she said.

"We need to go."

"We need some time. You're not strong enough."

I blinked back tears and let my shoulders fall. I knew she was right, but I garnered all of the strength I could and looked directly at her. "You know what it's like to be in the darkness. I know you remember. You saw what it did to my dad and I think that being under the influence of Lottie is even worse than Jacob." I furrowed my brow and wiped the rain from my face. "We can't leave them in there any longer."

Evie stared at her legs, the streetlamp lighting her profile. Her hair dripped water and hung in limp ringlets around her face. Then, she nodded. "Fine, St. Louis. We go now." She stood up and held out her hand.

I took it and pushed my tired body up from the bench. We stood for a moment under the tree.

"This feels like the end of something," she said quietly.

"Come on." I started across the square toward the west side of the city. We were walking against the wind and the going was tough. Sleet drove into our faces. Our already-wet clothes clung to us as we walked. Cars slid past, their headlights illuminating the sideways rain. We heard the highway before we saw it. Emerging from the alley that ran behind a church, we stood at the chain link fence along the northbound lanes. It was too late for many cars to be out, but semis thundered by, heading for the bridge that spanned the river.

Evie and I climbed the fence and slid down the other side, our feet landing in an icy puddle. We struggled up the embankment and stood on the shoulder. There were two lanes before the concrete divider and then two more lanes of traffic before the woods closed in on the other side.

"We'll have to run," Evie said, watching the trucks pass.

I nodded, my teeth chattering. We watched for a break in the traffic. The ground shook each time a truck passed, the speeding trailers creating eddies of frigid air that blew us around.

"Look," Evie pointed. "After this truck, there's nothing for a while. We'll go after it passes."

I nodded again, drawing upon my depleted reserves of energy with a deep breath. The truck sped past.

"Now!" Evie shouted. She darted across the highway, her feet splashing in the standing water.

I took off a second after her, chasing her form across the dark road. A moment later, lights hit us and I turned to see two semi-trucks barreling toward us from around the corner. As I turned, my shoe caught a slick spot and I went down. Hard. My shoulder crashed into the concrete and I cried out. Scrambling, I tried to find my feet. They slid and I couldn't get my balance. The trucks bore down on me.

"St. Louis!" Evie's voice was drowned out by the air horns of the trucks. The Jake brakes sounded staccato in the night.

I looked up at her. She was running back toward me.

"No!" I held my hand up and the air between us flexed. She was knocked back to the concrete barrier. I placed my hands on the pavement and pushed hard, launching myself up and running toward the middle of the highway.

The trucks passed, horns blaring as I reached the middle. Evie grabbed me and pulled me to her into a hug, our hair whipping around us.

"I thought..." Evie held me at arm's length.

"Let's go," I said, already looking up the other side.

The southbound lanes were much less busy and we could see farther up the road. It wasn't long before there was a long break in the traffic. We ran across the highway and climbed the fence on the other side, dropping into the scattered pine needles.

Evie leaned over, her hands on her knees. She was panting.

"Are you okay?"

She looked up at me. "That was really stupid."

I nodded. "And probably illegal." I could hear the wailing of a siren. "I'm sure someone's called it in already. Let's go."

We headed into the trees. Here, the majority of them were evergreens and their thick needles caught most of the rain before it reached us. It was a welcome reprieve. We made our way quickly through the tamped-down country, a soft bed of brush cushioning our steps. The trees passed alongside and I recognized the small creek running through the forest. It was exactly like the vision of Mr. Williams and Charlotte running through the forest the night they saved Mattie.

"Are you sure we're going the right way?" Evie asked at one point.

The locket burned against my skin as if in response. I nodded. "Yeah, I think so."

We walked along in silence until we reached the railroad tracks. The rain had finally stopped and as we stepped out from under the trees, the moon peeked out from behind a cloud. It bathed the dripping woods in a silver glow. I stood staring at the tracks, the wet rails glistening in the moonlight.

Evie stepped up beside me. "Is this it?"

"I think so," I whispered. Suddenly, the locket sprang to life and began burning. I placed a hand over it and grabbed Evie's with my free hand. I glanced over at her. "You ready?"

She smiled. "No."

We turned three times to the left and then once to the right. Twice. And a third time.

Nothing happened.

I wasn't sure what I had expected. I shook my head. It hadn't worked. Nothing about the night had changed. Except now, we were miles from the hotel. We were wet, tired, and cold. We had the locket but Andy, Tristan and Grant were being held by Lottie. And Mr. Williams was gone. Tears filled my eyes. Guilt washed over me.

"I'm so sorry. I don't know why it didn't work." I brought my free hand up and ran it across my eyes.

"Um, St. Louis?"

I looked over at Evie. She was standing next to me, but pointed in the other direction, looking at the path we had used to get to the railroad tracks. Her eyes were wide and she was staring straight ahead.

"You, um, might want to check this out, St. Louis,"

I whirled around.

There, in front of us, was the oldest tree I'd ever seen. Its branches were twisted and gnarled, the flaking bark gray under the moon. The roots spread down, shooting into the ground at odd angles. Among them was a small cabin. A lone circular window stood dark along the front wall. Nothing moved.

No one's home. I reached out; feeling for anything that would suggest Lottie was here. The place felt abandoned, quiet.

I looked over at Evie. "Do you see anything?"

"I don't see her color here. There are dozens of spikes, though. Oh, St. Louis. There are so many." She took her hand from mine and wrapped her arms across her chest. "Hmm, Mr. Williams was right."

"About what?"

"I can't see the cabin when I'm not holding your hand."

She held out her palm and I took it again. Mist rose up from the saturated ground as we walked, adding to the creepiness. Evie held my hand tightly. Hers was cold and clammy. The locket pressed against my chest and pulled simultaneously. It opened old wounds and the blood began to flow beneath the bandages Mr. Williams had placed there. I gritted my teeth against the pain.

A crow alit on a branch of the old tree and peered sideways at us as we crept toward the door. Its black eyes glinted in the moonlight. As we walked, the noises around us ceased and by the time we reached the door, the forest was silent.

"What now?" Evie whispered.

I swallowed and shook my head.

The crow cried out and I jumped nearly out of my skin. My hand shaking, I reached up and tried the latch on the door, scraping old wood with my knuckles. Nothing happened. I reached up again, but something held me back. I grunted and tried to knock on the door again.

"They know what you're going to do," Evie whispered.

I looked over at her and then at my hand. The moonlight illuminated it with a silvery light. The green and purple veins pulsed beneath my skin, holding my hand inches from making contact with the door. Anger shot through me and I used every last bit of energy to break their hold on me. My hand came down so hard on the door that the skin split on my knuckles. An oily noise from inside wound its way through the crack under the door. It was like someone dragging a decomposing body across the floorboards. I shook my head to rid it of the image. Evie whimpered and tried to pull me away from the door, but my feet were rooted to the ground. The sound intensified in the silent forest and then stopped. The quietness pressed in on us.

Then, the door opened.

I stood, my face mere inches from Lottie. Her cracked lips drew up into a smile, revealing decaying teeth. A smell like a rotting animal on the side of the highway rose up from her and it was all I could do to keep from retching.

"Welcome, Marisssaaa," she hissed.

I gathered my energy to run. Evie pulled at me, her eyes white all the way around the irises and her face drawn tight in terror. I had just turned when I felt something grab me from behind. Talons pressed into the tender flesh of my shoulder and I cried out. The moment froze and I felt it all. All of the pain and sadness and hopelessness. The only thing I did in that moment was close and open my eyes. When I opened them, we were inside the cabin and things were happening around me, but I couldn't process them all at once. It was too much.

The noise was the first thing I processed. Evie screaming. The wind rushing through the towering trees outside. The crow cawing at the window. The sound of something ripping. The sound of the locket being pulled from its place on my chest.

The pain was the next thing I processed. The open wound on my chest. My knuckles dripping blood. And the ripping. Like I was being torn in half.

Suddenly, everything stopped and I blinked. I was floating above the floor of the cabin. A cloaked figure stood over two bodies. One was an old woman that was nothing more than a skeleton, the bones crumbling to dust in the wind. The other was my best friend. The cloaked figure held the locket in her gnarled hands. She pulled a wisp of light away from Evie's body and sent it careening into a jar on the shelf. It spun there, banging against the sides of the jar. She placed a candle on top and lit the wick. A wisp of smoke trailed along the floor and then crept up into the jar, wrapping itself around the light, extinguishing it as the wax cascaded down the sides.

The figure flicked its wrist and Evie sat up, her eyes hollow as she stared up at the figure. Another flick of the wrist and Evie stood. She swayed slightly and then began walking toward the door, her movements jerky.

I tried to cry out. When I did, the figure looked up and her hood fell away. It took me a moment to realize that I was looking at my own face, the eyes black pits of evil. Her mouth, *my mouth,* twisted into a smile. The pain intensified and I couldn't catch my breath. She brought a hand up and swept it down, the energy between us arcing. A hit like a sledgehammer slammed into my chest. Another ripping sound and part of me was yanked away. It glowed, colors swirling as it moved through the air toward Lottie. It landed on her chest and stuck there.

The last thing I processed was the darkness. It was all-encompassing and absolute.

The darkness was the last thing I processed.

Chapter 21

My hand was wet.

I tried to open my eyes, but they wouldn't respond. Water lapped at my hand and I forced my eyelids open. I lay face-down on the edge of a lake. It was nighttime. The only sound I could pick up was the sound of the water moving along the shoreline. Everything inside me hurt. It took a couple of tries, but I was finally able to push up into a sitting position. The moon reflected on the lake's surface, bathing everything around me in a silvery glow. I swallowed, my throat burning with the action. The dirt underneath me was cold. My ears hurt with the silence around me. I breathed in once, twice, trying to center myself. It didn't work.

It was all off. I felt dizzy and I closed my eyes.

Grant. Andy. Tristan. Evie.

What happened to them? I had to get to them, to save them.

I opened my eyes and looked down at my knuckles. The skin was pristine. No split skin where I had hit the door. I reached up to touch my chest. A hole where something had been and now was not. I tried to breathe as I pressed at the empty space. *The locket. Jacob. Mattie.* Lottie had the locket. She had my friends. She had part of *me.* It was all over. I had charged in to save my friends and I had ruined everything. A tear ran down my cheek as I stood up on shaky legs, and then turned to look at my surroundings.

I was on an island. The trees bent under the moonlight, their leaves moving in the slight breeze. Underbrush and grass spread to the waterline. I reached out and ran a hand over the grass that was matted where I had lain. The grass was brown and dead. I stood up again and wrapped my arms around me.

I walked around the island three times, looking for a bridge or a boat. Nothing. The water spread out around me as far as I could see, like glass reflecting the moonlight. I returned to where I started and sat. The walk had exhausted me and I rested my head on my knees.

"Marissa, I want you to be ready to let me go."

My head shot up. "Mom?"

"I'm ready to go now."

There, on the surface of the water, playing like a movie on a screen was my mother. I cried out and covered my mouth with my hand. She was lying on the hospital bed in our house in Creve Coeur. The sunlight shone in through the front windows, spreading along the white sheets on her bed. She smiled and held out her hand. I saw myself walk into the frame and take it. I remembered this day. It was the last time I'd seen her alive.

My heart split for a moment, tearing my insides apart. I watched my mother long after the memory of myself had gone to bed. I watched as my dad walked in and held her hand, talking softly to her as she coughed and begged for more pain medication. I watched as she took shallow breaths, one after another, until finally, her chest was unmoving. I watched as her head fell to the side, the morning sun lighting up her features as she left her body.

The moment of my mother's death replayed over and over until I put my head in my hands to stop it. I rocked back and forth, trying not to hear the sound of her begging my dad to let her go. After what seemed like hours or days, the sound stopped. The sudden silence was deafening and it made me think I was going crazy.

I looked up.

Grant. Andy. Evie. Who else? Wasn't there someone else I should remember?

I blinked. It was still nighttime and the water of the lake was quiet again. The relief was overwhelming but short-lived. A moment after I opened my eyes, the surface of the lake shimmered again and I saw my dad. He was running through the woods behind our house.

Grandpa's voice followed him out the door. "Hurry. Marissa's in trouble."

Dad slipped his way down to the cave entrance. He managed to move some of the rocks from the cave-in and squeezed through the hole he created.

"Marissa!" he shouted into the darkness. Something moved in the back corner. "Peanut?" he said quieter.

Dad made his way toward the back of the cave, toward the black thing hunched in the corner. I tried to call out to tell him to go back and that it wasn't me, but he couldn't hear me. He crept up to the black thing and reached out with a trembling hand. The thing turned and latched onto him, yanking him through the labyrinth of tunnels under the town. He screamed as his shoulder was bashed against the rock walls. When he got to the cavern, the black smoke pulled him in, caressing his face with its evil tendrils. Dad's eyes turned blank and he was pushed to the ground by the smoke. It shackled him and began to twist his memories.

I leaned closer to the water as I saw what he saw.

He was standing at Evie's bedside at the hospital. Except, it wasn't Evie in the bed. It was me. He choked on his sobs as the heart monitor flat-lined. I turned away, my hands over my ears, trying to block out the sound of my dad crying. The sound finally faded and the image played again.

As I stood there, watching the images play over and over on the surface of the water, a small spark ignited within me and I got angry. I stood up and started looking for a rock. Almost as if it appeared from nowhere, a rock was at my feet. I picked it up and flung it with all my might at the surface of the water. It hit with a *kerplunk* and sent ripples out, distorting the image of my dad being dragged through the cave. It stopped and I let a smile turn the corners of my mouth. I turned away from the water and started up the bank. A voice behind me stopped me in my tracks.

"Marissa, I want you to be ready to let me go."

"Marissa!"

"Hey, St. Louis, I'm going to be fine, really."

"Help me, Marissa!"

"She's burning! My God almighty, she's burning!"

"Ugísa^n!"

The blood ran cold in my veins as the voices filled my senses. I stood, my back ramrod straight, fear coursing through me. The voices rose into the night and I knew even before I turned that this was not going to be good.

The ripples had spread out, shattering the surface of the water into several smaller screens, each playing a memory. Evie's mother hitting her. Andy and Tristan fighting. MingkéHá being dragged down into the prairie. Sam watching Sarah burn. Amalie trying to find her way through the forest in the snow. Hans trying to get out of the fire. Mary pulling Matthias' lifeless body from the bridge. Theodore shooting himself. Duncan being kidnapped. Dad being dragged through the caves. My mother dying.

Grant. Evie. Someone else...someone else?

I backed away from the water, my mouth open.

"No, no, no, no, no," I whispered over and over again.

Whipping around, I ran from the memories, the sounds of people in pain. I pounded straight across the middle of the island. The brambles and underbrush reached up to tangle around my legs as I ran. I got to the other side and slid down the bank to the shore. The voices were quieter here and the water was blissfully tranquil.

For a moment.

The ripples made their way around the island, their voices pounding into me. Breaking everything in me.

"I tried to help you all!" I screamed. "I tried!"

A sound like a wounded animal came from my core and I threw my head up to the moon above, allowing all of the anguish to find a voice, to spread out into the night. And, then I cried. I cried for my mom, my dad, my grandparents, Sam, Jacob, and Evie. I cried for all of them, the sobs wracking my body with pain. I had lost everyone, *everyone* that had ever meant anything to me.

It was too much. I was broken.

"I can't!" I collapsed on the ground, not caring that mud was seeping into my clothes and that it had begun to rain. The voices amped up in volume and I curled into a ball. I wrapped my arms around my middle. I wanted it to stop. I forgot myself in that time. I was no longer Marissa and there was no longer anything else but the voices and the pain.

My grandma's story came floating back to me across the miles:

Long ago, there were two brothers. When they grew up and got married, they each built houses on the banks of a large lake near our town. The eldest son's wife coveted the younger brother and told her husband that he had cheated her out of her share of the family's wheat. When the eldest brother found out about this, he took his younger brother out to the middle of the lake on a fishing trip. When they got to the island, the younger brother began fishing and when he wasn't looking, the eldest brother got back in the boat and rowed away, leaving the little brother to die alone on the island.

We all die alone, Marissa.

I was going to die on this island.

Alone.

I don't know how long I lay there, my sobs turning from gulps to hiccups. When my hand fell from my middle and lay open on the ground, I stared at it. It didn't even feel like it was part of me. The rain stopped and the moon came out from behind a cloud. The ground and my hand were illuminated in its glow. I furrowed my brow and looked at my hand again. The hand that held my mother's that last night. The hand that had held onto Evie and kept her from drowning. The hand that Grant held and kissed while he was driving. The hand that had allowed Melanie to see Red. The hand that had helped my dad move the furniture into our new home.

My hand.

I drew it into a fist. *My hand.*

As I sat up, I looked at the memory closest to me. In it, MingkéHá was being killed and drawn down into the ground and to the cavern below over and over. He screamed. The sound brought tears afresh to my eyes. I crept closer to the water.

"No," I said as I reached out and touched the surface of the black water. A ripple spread out from my fingertip. As it touched the edge of the memory, it changed. In the memory, MingkéHá passed his powers to Sam and turned to see his wife. They embraced and walked away, together. The memory faded away and left a blank spot in the water. I took a cleansing breath, energy shooting through my limbs.

It wasn't blank for long, though. In its place, another memory floated over. In this one, Amalie wandered through the woods behind her house, tripping over the underbrush with bare feet frozen by the snow. She wandered around until she fell over a huge log and lay in the snow.

I took a shaky breath and touched the water. The ripples spread until they touched the edge and then, I saw all of us there. We were in the woods behind Hannah's house. I sat on the ground next to her. My voice filled the space, drowning out the others for a moment.

"You're not alone now, Amalie. We're here. You're not alone."

A smile played on her lips as she looked past me. My figure wavered and then disappeared and those of my friends did as well. Amalie stood up from her body and stared at something behind a tree. It was Hans. He stepped forward and pulled her into a hug. They walked back to the house, holding hands.

Amalie chattered to her brother the whole time. "Da war eine...*lady.* Sie war nett."

This was how I spent the next hours, or days, or however long it took. Time did not seem to matter here. With each change, I felt myself grow stronger, more *me.* Each memory faded until I stood on the bank looking at the two remaining ones.

In one, bodies lay in a garden. I didn't quite recognize them. Or did I? I rubbed my hand over my eyes and tried to concentrate. I turned my attention to the other memory. In it, my mother was telling me to let her go. I stared at that one for a long time and then pressed my finger to the black water. The ripple seemed to hesitate, as if it didn't want to leave the safety of the bank. When it finally reached the memory, it began to glow around the edges.

I blinked and squinted at the water. My mother was there. We were all there. We were at the family reunion in Troy, and Mom was laughing in her lawn chair. My eyes filled with tears as I watched her laugh, the wrinkles overcoming her eyes. I missed that sound more than anything. The memories began to loop repeatedly in rapid succession. In one, Mom and I were baking cookies and I jumped when she dropped a pan. The motion sent the open bottle of sprinkles in my hand all across the kitchen floor. We laughed. In another, my mom was reading to a small version of me. I was lying on her lap under Grandma's afghan. As my mother read, her fingers gently swept the hair back from my temples and forehead.

I reached up and touched the place where I could almost feel her fingers. A smile worked its way up as I watched the memory change to the time I got roller skates for Christmas. Mom put them on and rolled down the hallway in her bathrobe, hooting with laughter the whole way. The next memory was when I won the spelling bee at school. I looked out into the crowd and saw my mom. She was smiling and clapping louder than anyone.

You can stay here forever, you know.

I looked around to find the source of the voice then shook my head. I recognized it as my own.

I want to. I want to see my mom every single day.

They're just memories.

I blinked back tears. A journal full of memories of my mother sat on the closet shelf in my room back home. Pages filled with times we spent together.

But, they were just words, cold and static.

These are better. They're memories of her. They're all I have left. If I stay here, I'll never forget her. I'll get to stay with her forever.

The other voice in my head was quiet for a moment as I stared at the memory of my mom and me riding in the car. We were listening to the Black Crowes at top volume with the windows rolled down, the summer air lifting my hair as I put my hand out the window, letting it dance on the wind.

I sniffed.

I miss her.

It won't bring her back.

I sat on the bank and brought my knees up to my chest. I knew it wouldn't bring her back, but the sound of her voice, her laughter, filled a hole in my soul that I'd almost forgotten was there. I would watch one more. One more.

Mom and I walking and talking.

Mom and I shopping.

Mom and I cooking.

Mom and I.

Mom.

Mom.

"I miss you. Every single day." I stood up and took a deep breath. "But, I don't need this anymore. I have it all in here." I pressed my hand to my heart. "I have all of these memories here."

Are you sure?

I stared at the memories and drew in a cool breath of night air. It centered me.

I'm sure.

I knelt at the water's edge, my finger hovering above the surface. A breeze blew gentle across my cheek and I closed my eyes. I lowered my finger to the water. The sounds of the memories began to fade. The last thing I heard was my mother laughing, then silence.

I sat with my eyes closed for a long time. When I opened them, she was gone.

But, not really.

I placed my hand on my chest and stood up. I felt stronger than I'd felt since leaving Culvers Grove. I stared at the last memory. It floated to the bank, and as I stared, some of the faces came into focus and I remembered. My friends!

Andy! Tristan! Grant! Evie!

Recognition slammed into me and I paced along the lake's edge. I had to help my friends!

Taking a deep breath, I reached to the water and let my finger hover an inch above the surface.

A moment before I made contact, the water in the middle of the memory boiled. I skittered back, landing on my rear end.

I watched in horror as a hand reached out of the water toward me.

CHAPTER 22

I pushed away from the water along the ground, my backside scraping mud with it. I stared wide-eyed at the hand as it groped the air above the lake. My legs weren't working and I scrambled up the embankment, trying to get my feet under me on the slippery grass. I turned to look behind me, certain that the hand was going to grab me and drag me below the surface. As I turned, though, something about the hand made me freeze. I tilted my head and looked hard. Something about it was familiar. Comforting.

"Grant!" I clamored back down the bank to the water. The memory had drifted close to the bank and I learned out over the surface, looking at the memory. My friends' bodies lay on the ground, but the center of the memory was open. I smiled as I looked into the opening. Grant reached his hand up through the water.

"How did you find me?"

Grant smiled. "I saw you in the reflection."

I blinked and looked up at the moon. Then, I reached out for Grant's hand.

He wrapped his fingers around mine and smiled. "Hold on tight."

There was an overpowering pulling sensation and I was moving along in the darkness. I panicked for a moment. *Was this one of Lottie's tricks?* Light from a circle above me lit up the walls and I saw the wind moving around, like the dream I had where I saw my parents meet for the first time. Grant's hand stayed strong, holding on to me and guiding me toward him.

I landed hard, my legs almost scorpioning over my head.

"Marissa!" Grant ran to me and knelt, gathering me in his arms. They didn't seem to wrap quite all the way around me but they felt nice, comforting.

I hugged him back and cried as he held me. "I'm so glad you're here."

"I thought I lost you forever." Grant kissed the top of my head and held me to him again, the feeling of something missing haunting me. "Where were you?"

I took a deep breath. "I think Lottie thought she would be able to break me by putting me on that island. It was supposed to be like when people went into the smoke, the blackness. It showed me all of these awful memories, but I realized that they weren't inherently bad. They turned into good ones and I, um, got to say goodbye to my mom."

Grant grazed a hand along my cheek. "You're so brave." He kissed me, his lips a whisper on my own.

I looked up when his lips left mine. "Where are we?"

"I have no idea." He stood up and held out his hand.

I took his hand and let him leverage me from the ground. His hand kept slipping and it took a few times, but I finally got to my feet. I looked around. Shelves lined the walls, filled with earthen jugs, herbs, and glass jars with candle wax covering the tops and dripping down the sides. Within the glass jars, bits of light danced around, like lightning bugs. A fire burned in the fireplace, casting an eerie orange glow in the space. I moved and scanned the room. A pile of dust lay on the floor. Something nagged at the edge of my mind. I shook my head.

"We're in her cabin," I breathed, walking toward the middle of the room.

"Careful," Grant warned a second before I ran into an invisible barrier. "Sorry."

I stood, running my hands along the barrier. It spread out on my left and right and as high as I could reach. "What is this?"

"We're in a jar. Like the others on the shelves."

I ran my hands along the glass, my eyes scanning through the shelves. I caught a small movement from the shelf near the fireplace. I squinted. There, in a jar near the top shelf was Andy. He stood at the glass wall, waving at me.

"Andy!" I shouted, relief pounding through my core.

"Wait, can you hear Andy again? In your head?"

I shook my head absently, waving furiously at Andy.

"You should be able to, right?"

I stopped moving and looked at Grant, something dancing around the periphery of my consciousness. "What?"

"Try to talk to him in your mind." Grant nodded toward Andy's shelf. "He's higher up than us. He can see what's on top of the jar, holding us in. Then he can tell you."

"Right." *Andy, can you hear me?*

Nothing in response.

"I can't hear him through the glass." I turned to look at the rest of the cabin. "Is Tristan here, too?"

Grant pointed.

I stared out through the glass at the shelves across the cabin from us. Tristan sat in the middle of his jar, his knees drawn up to his chest. He was rocking back and forth, tears streaming down his cheeks. I realized that from his angle, he couldn't see Andy's jar. *Did he even know he was alive?*

"Tristan!" I shouted. "Andy's fine!"

Grant placed a hand on my shoulder. "He can't hear you. I've tried."

Despair washed over me and I leaned against the jar for support. As I did, my line of sight took in the floor below. "Grant? Where's Evie?" Icicles shot down my arms and my insides cramped.

"Lottie took Evie with her." Grant licked his lips. "Before she did, she pulled a light or something out of her and put it in there."

Something nagged at my memory as I followed his finger with my eyes and saw a dark jar on the low shelf near the door. Black smoke whirled around inside. A vision, murky and muddled fought its way around my head.

"We have to get out of here," Grant said, pacing the space like a caged animal. "Maybe if we push the jar enough, we can get it to roll off the shelf?" Grant took a running start and jammed his shoulder into the side of the jar. Nothing happened. No movement at all. He did it again and again. The jar didn't budge.

I stood staring at him as he threw himself full force into the glass. Something was coalescing in my mind. "Grant," I placed a gentle hand on his arm as he prepared to shuttle himself at the side again. "How's your shoulder?"

Grant furrowed his brow and pivoted his arm around a couple of times. "Feels fine."

"Don't you think you should have moved the jar or hurt yourself by now?"

He looked into my eyes. "What are you getting at?"

"How are we small enough to be in this jar, Grant? And, how are you not feeling any pain even after throwing your shoulder into the glass twenty times?"

He stared at me.

"We're souls," I whispered. "Ghosts."

Grant blinked several times and then shook his head. "No, we're in some sort of a glass enclosure and we have to find our way out."

I put more pressure on his arm with my hand. "Look," I said as my hand passed through his arm. "She trapped our souls in these jars," I mumbled, running my hands along the glass surface. Then I turned to Grant. "Grant, she was taking spirits and keeping them in jars."

Like lightning bugs.

CHAPTER 23

"Ghosts," Grant mumbled without turning around. "She trapped all of them?"

I walked over and stood next to him. His eyes scanned the shelves upon shelves of jars with figures and lights inside, some moving, some not.

"Why?" he breathed.

I shook my head. "She's broken. Something in her is broken and she wants everyone else to hurt as much as she does."

"That's twisted."

"We have to get out of here." I heard a bump somewhere in the cabin and I froze. "What was that?"

Grant stopped moving and put an ear to the glass. "I heard it, too. There it is again."

We scanned the room, looking for anything that could be making that sound.

"Look!" I shouted.

Below, Tristan was running at the side of the jar, throwing his shoulder against the side. I threw my arms up and waved them. "Stop! You can't move it!"

He didn't see me and kept running at the wall.

"Did you see that?"

I looked over at Grant. "What?"

"His jar's moving!"

"That's impossible."

"Well, it's happening. Look, a little bit each time."

Tristan threw himself at the jar and it moved. A tiny bit, but it moved. Each hit caused the bottom of the jar to slide forward on the shelf. It seemed like days, but finally, it teetered, halfway on and halfway off.

I looked up at Andy's jar. He was watching, transfixed.

Suddenly, a jar crashed to the floor, shaking me from my thoughts. Tristan sprang up and started rifling through the jars on the shelf. He got to ours and peered at us. Smiling, he brought his hands up and placed them on either side of the jar. He bit his bottom lip, concentrating and brought the jar forward until it fell from the shelf. It shattered on the ground and Grant and I stepped out. Grant gathered me into a hug. His arms passed through me. He stared down at them.

"Where's Andy?" Tristan asked, his eyes red-rimmed. "I don't see Andy."

I pointed to Andy's jar. Glass shattered and Andy and Tristan held onto each other.

"Miss me?" Andy asked.

Tristan nodded, and then placed his hands on either side of Andy's face. "You're real. You're here and you're real."

Andy nodded, a tear rolling down his cheek. "I'm here."

"We have to help Evie." I searched the shelves for Evie's jar and finally found it on the lowest shelf near the door. The black smoke whirled around inside, almost obscuring the small form of Evie's soul. She lay in the middle of the jar, her knees tucked up to her chest. I grabbed again and again at the jar, my hands passing through it each time. "Tristan, she's here!"

Tristan walked over and knelt. He took a deep breath and placed his hands on either side of the jar.

"We're ghosts. We can't affect the real world." My voice was small. "I don't understand."

Tristan looked up at me. "I'm part of the club now. Poltergeist. I can move things in the real world even if I'm a spirit."

"How did you..." My voice faded. The dream came rushing back. "Except it wasn't a dream was it?"

"I'm sorry," Tristan said. "I had to get to Andy."

"What's going on?" Grant asked.

"After he saw that you got some of my powers by touching the locket, he touched it so he could get to Andy. Can you get her out?" I asked.

Grant stood beside me and shook his head. "Why is there smoke in her jar?"

"Lottie's punishing her," I bit my bottom lip, "for pulling me away earlier."

Grant placed his hand on my shoulder. It was a whisper, but I could feel it and it gave me strength. Tristan concentrated on the jar and moved it to the edge.

"What are you going to do with the smoke?" Grant's eyes held so much worry that it made me choke up.

"We're going to trap it in another jar," I said. "I'll hold onto it and Tristan can close it in." I turned to Tristan. "Light a candle and trap it inside."

He nodded.

As soon as the jar broke on the floor, everything started moving all at once. The smoke shot out, aimed directly at me. It hit me like a freight train and I tried to grab hold of it. It slipped out of my hands, leaving them with an oily residue coating them. I made a mad grab for it again and finally caught hold of it. It spun around, trying to get at me, like a snake striking the air near my face. I held it out from me, stepping back from the table as it fought against my grasp.

"She won't come out," Andy said to Tristan.

I glanced down. Evie sat in the middle of the shattered glass, her knees drawn up to her chest.

"Evie!" I shouted.

The smoke took the opportunity, yanked itself from my grasp, and shot at Grant. I cried out and lunged at it, catching it a moment before it got to Grant. It was then that I heard Evie crying.

"Evie! It's safe! We're all here!"

The smoke changed tactics and began beating against me, taking chunks of my soul and sending them out into the room. They floated for a moment and then shot back to me, almost sliding back into place, but not quite.

Grant rushed at me. "Leave her alone!"

Evie sprang up and put herself in between us, blocking Grant from moving.

"It's killing her!" he shouted.

"Put the smoke in here," Tristan said. He stood next to me, the wick lit in his hand and a jar in the other.

I struggled to put it in the jar. It didn't want to go and fought hard against me. I pulled all the energy I could and forced it into the jar.

"Put the lid on, Tristan!"

Tristan slammed the lid closed and held it tight while the candle melted on top, dripping wax over the lid and down the sides. The smoke careened around the jar, banging against the lid, but it couldn't get out.

I whipped around and looked for Evie. "Are you okay?" I scanned her up and down but didn't see any damage to her spirit.

She smiled. "It'll take a lot more than that to take me out, St. Louis. It just took me a minute to find my way back." Her eyes swept down to the floor. "Hey, where's my body?"

"Lottie took it."

She shook her head. "Sounds like it's time to get it back."

"You think she's..."

"I think she's gone home for a wedding."

CHAPTER 24

"Wedding?"

Evie shrugged. "She has everything she needs now to be with Jacob forever."

"How do you know all of this?" I asked, tilting my head.

She smiled. "I watched her through the smoke. She thought it would break me but she was wrong this time."

I nodded. "I know what you mean."

"She took the locket and put it around her, um, your neck and then she stood over my body. It sat up and blinked and then looked up at her, but the eye sockets were black." She shuddered. "It was the creepiest thing I've ever seen, St. Louis. It was like my body was a puppet and she was using the smoke as the strings. She left. In your body, dragging mine with her."

As she spoke, the memory slammed into me. "She's going to the house to bind him to her," I whispered.

"We need to get your bodies back," Andy said.

Not going to be that easy. She has part of me.

Andy squinted at me. "I can't hear you. Are you talking to me?"

I bit my bottom lip. "She has part of me," I said quietly.

"What do you mean she has part of you, Anderson?"

I shook my head. "She took part of my soul so that she could be with Jacob." I placed my hand over the hole in my chest and pulled my shirt collar up a bit.

Grant grabbed my hand and looked into my eyes. "Why didn't you tell me?"

I shook my head. "It's no big deal. She needed the part of me that allows me to walk between the worlds. With that, she can bind Jacob to her and exist. In *this* world."

"She won't ever die," Evie breathed.

"Wait, wait. I don't understand," Grant took a step away. "Why is Charlotte doing all this?"

"Not Charlotte," Evie said, holding his gaze, "Ottolie."

"Who's that?" Andy asked.

"Lottie, Charlotte's cousin," I said. "We met someone, um, Mr. Williams, who knew Lottie when she was alive. He told us about how evil she was."

Between us, Evie and I filled the boys in on everything Mr. Williams had told us and about how we got to the cabin.

"She's been borrowing bodies?" Tristan asked. "Like a zombie?"

I nodded. "She used dark magic to exist in other's bodies. Until she could get to me."

Grant stared at me for a minute. "Fine. She has part of your soul and all of our bodies. What do we do now?"

I noticed a tremor in his voice. He was as scared as I was. I turned to Evie. "Ideas?"

"She'll be at the house," Evie said with confidence.

I didn't disagree with her. "That's exactly where she'll be. How is she going to bind Jacob to her?"

"First, she'll have to break him. Like she broke Charlotte. Lottie sent a letter to Charlotte that told her that Jacob had found someone else and that he no longer wanted her or the child. It broke her heart.

She's going to have to tell Jacob the same thing. Once he agrees to marry her, what then?" she asked.

Tristan had broken off from the group and was poring over a stack of books on the table near the door to the back of the cabin. He looked up when the room got quiet.

"Oh," he said. "It's right here. The binding spell." He pointed to the largest of the books. We gathered around and stared at it.

"This is some dark stuff," Andy said. "You said Mr. Williams taught her Hoodoo?"

I shook my head. "She stole a journal from him that he was using to make potions, but she took it to a darker place."

"Black magic," Tristan said, running his fingers over the handwritten pages. They crinkled under his touch. He glanced up. "I did a paper in history last year."

"What is the binding spell?"

Tristan scanned down the list of instructions. "She already has everything else she needs. She's going to bind his soul to hers through this incantation."

"We need to go in with a plan," Evie said.

I didn't miss that she looked directly at me as she said it.

"If she's at the house, then the only one who will be able to see it will be Marissa," Tristan said.

"Not necessarily. We're all, well, ghosts, so we can see the real world *and* the spirit world," I said.

Andy smiled. "We'll be like the great Anderson, then."

"Basically. That's why we're all able to see this place right now. No one living would be able to find it walking by. It's like a, um, a..." I searched for the word.

"A trick?"

"A mirage?"

Evie smiled. "An overlay. It's where the barrier is so thin that it perfectly overlays the real world beneath it."

"Right!" I felt my cheeks fill with heat. "We'll all be able to see the house."

"So freaking weird, Anderson."

I stopped and swallowed. "I didn't even ask. I-I mean I assumed you would all be willing to, but, but..."

Andy took Tristan's hand. "She wants to know if we're all in."

Tristan stared at me for a minute, emotions playing across his face in rapid succession. Finally, he squeezed Andy's hand. "I'm in."

Andy nodded and then turned to me. "We're all in, Anderson."

I took a deep breath and looked over at Grant. "She's got the locket, which means she has Jacob."

"And Mattie," Evie offered. "Do you think she knows that Mattie is in there with Jacob?"

I shook my head. "I don't think so. There's no reason she should be in there with him."

"Can she see inside the locket?"

"No. I think she could see through it when it was open, but now that it's closed, she thinks it's only Jacob in there."

"It's going to take all of us to overpower her," Evie said.

Tristan smiled and nodded toward me. "I think we were wrong about who was giving the powers through the locket. I don't think Lottie had anything to do with the powers that Grant and I got from you. I think that they came from Mattie, Jacob, and you especially. The locket had tapped into the part of your soul that was ripped out when Lottie took the locket. It was connected to the part that makes you, well, able to do what you do."

"So, what we got was stronger than what Evie or Andy got, more, um, potent?" Grant asked.

Tristan nodded. "Lottie is strong, but she was only able to use the locket as a cursed object. She didn't have control over it. When it was open, it pulled people to the cavern under the town."

"Then, what kept them all there? Where's the barrier coming from?"

I shook my head. "I don't know. I do know that we can't do anything to help Culvers Grove without stopping Lottie first." I felt weak.

"How are you?" Grant asked.

"Um, I'm tired. Feeling a bit weak." I rubbed my hand over my eyes and then held his again.

"You look lighter, like you're fading a bit." His eyes were full of concern.

"I'm fine, really," I said. The truth was, I felt like I was sinking in quicksand. I was tired. So very tired.

"So, we go to the abandoned building across town and then what?"

I tried to focus on what the group was planning.

"It's going to be the house as it was for the wedding," Evie said. "She's going to have the wedding that she believed should have been hers."

A twinge of something sad pricked at my heart. "You know, she's not that much different from me. She lost her mother and felt so alone."

"But you didn't become a psycho."

I shot Andy a half-smile. "It's still sad."

"Are you telling us that you feel sorry for her? That's crazy. She took all of these people's souls and kept them. She hurt so many people from Culvers Grove. Sam, Amalie, Mary..." With each name,

Tristan's voice amped up a bit. "And now she wants to steal your body and marry Jacob? What's wrong with you, Marissa?"

I pressed my lips together. "She was sad and lonely."

Tristan gave Andy a look and shook his head. "I don't get it."

"She's not saying that we aren't going to take her down, she's simply saying that she can understand what drove her to do those things." Andy leaned over and bumped Tristan with his shoulder. "Give her a break, okay?"

Tristan's eyes continued to hold a fire in them, but he quieted and stood stoic at Andy's side. "What are we going to do?"

"We have to return Mattie and Jacob to Charlotte. She's been trapped in that house for years. If we can put their family back together, then Jacob won't marry Lottie." I looked around at the group. "I don't know how we're going to get the locket from her, though."

"Can we overpower her?"

"Maybe distract her?"

"Run at her and take her out?"

I realized that Grant had let go of my hand and had wandered to the door next to the fireplace. It was nearly hidden by strings of dried herbs and flowers. He walked through and then called to us from behind the door.

Andy followed. "Holy crap," he said, stepping into the room beyond.

We followed him, arcing out into a half circle around the table standing in the center of the room. On the table was an enormous glass cover, like one on the cake stand my mother used to have on her counter. She never put a cake in it, but it was an antique and she said she liked the way it looked. A layer of dust covered the glass. Tristan wiped his hand across it, smearing the dust but allowing a glimpse inside.

I leaned closer. "Is that..."

Tristan grabbed a piece of cloth from a pile on the floor and proceeded to wipe away the majority of the dust.

"What is this?" Grant breathed.

"It's Culvers Grove. The whole flipping town." Evie placed a hand on the glass and quickly drew it back. "There's a spike over it, like the real place." She held out her hand to me and I took it, holding onto her so my legs wouldn't give out.

There, within the glass enclosure was the town square. I could even make out Jessica's Jeep parked near the diner. The town hall stood in the center, lights appearing in the upper windows. I followed the road out of town and along the hills and curves of the country. There was the farm. My dad's car. My car. Lights on in the house. Sadness coating the walls. I drew a sharp breath in. Hot tears built behind my eyes.

"That's why no one could leave. She was keeping them all here."

Andy stared at table, unmoving. A tear dripped from the corner of his eye and ran down his cheek. "My mom, my dad, my sister. My *family*."

Tristan tried to place a hand on Andy's shoulder but he shrugged it off.

"She was keeping them all here."

"Still feel sorry for her, Marissa?"

CHAPTER 25

Twenty minutes later, we were making our way under the highway near the canal a half mile up from where Evie and I made our treacherous crossing earlier that evening. Once on the other side, the city of Savannah lay quiet like a moss-covered monster slumbering in the silvery moonlight. We crept along the alleys and sidewalks, meeting no one. It was as if the city was holding its breath. Silence pressed down on us as we walked, single file, bodiless sentries. My senses were on overload as I tried to feel for anything that would lead us to danger. I was fading with each step and I concentrated on moving along the wet, slushy sidewalks.

"She's there," Evie breathed when we walked into Ogelthorpe Square. She pointed to the area of sky visible through the tree branches. "I see a huge spike up there."

"It could be just Charlotte," I said. The ramification of not seeing Lottie's spike was not going unnoticed by me.

She shook her head. "I can see Charlotte's, but there's another one there. It's darker somehow, more sinister. And it pokes up more."

She held out her hand. I took it.

"She hasn't completely taken over your body yet, St. Louis."

I nodded and let her hand fall. "Let's keep going."

We made our way around the corner and stood in a line at the end of the alleyway, staring along the street at the spectral house that stood, tucked neatly between a tattoo parlor and a bookstore. The wrought iron that outlined the windows and trees shone dully in the sunlight and a warm breeze wound its way to us, beckoning us forward with the promise of summer.

Evie reached out and took my hand with her left and Andy's with her right. He took Tristan's and Tristan took Grant's. We were all together, bonded by our shared journey, our shared goal, and by our friendship. I swallowed around the lump in my throat as I considered for a moment all that my friends had done for me. They had followed me into the fire time and time again, and here they were, willing to put their lives on the line for us. My center filled with strength, garnered from the energy passing right to left between us all.

"You ready?" Evie whispered.

I nodded, my eyes never leaving the house. "I'm ready."

She dropped my hand and started up the street. We were twenty feet from the front yard when I saw it. Evie saw it at about the same time and nodded toward it. The smoke hung in sheets a bit above the grass, almost blending in, a sinister blanket lying in wait for some unsuspecting soul to step into it. It boiled and undulated, a trap set by Lottie to keep intruders out.

I crept around the side of the building and Evie settled behind me, kneeling.

"Do you have them?" she asked Tristan.

He came up and held out his hand, a candle and matches held within. He placed them on the sidewalk next to us. "Grant and Andy went to look for a container. I'll be back."

"It's so much," I whispered, looking at the black mist. "What if I can't hold onto all of it?"

Tristan came back, straining to carry a large jar. He was using every bit of concentration and determination to get it over to the sidewalk without breaking it. Finally, he set it down, the glass bottom grinding a bit on the pavement.

"It was from the bar next door," Andy said.

"It smells like olives." Evie wrinkled her nose.

"Better than the pickled eggs container next to it in the recycling can."

Grant was next to me then, his hand pressing down on mine, or rather, I noticed, pressing through mine. He looked at it, too, and then back up at me, his eyes showing surprise but quickly recovering. His voice was unwavering. "I'm here. You don't have to do this alone."

I shook my head. "No, I don't want it to hurt you."

"I've got your back."

I blinked and then stood up and faced the smoke, reaching out to it with my energy, touching it gently with a whisper. It responded immediately, shooting into a small area that was darkness incarnate. It approached slowly, carefully. I wondered if it knew I wasn't alone.

"Come on," I whispered. "Come on."

It drew up above me, high in the air and came slamming down, crushing me into the pavement. I cried out and grabbed wildly as it pummeled me into the street again and again. It began taking bites of my soul, and this time, it was hungry. I felt parts of me being ripped away and floating back. I grabbed onto it with my hands, arms, wrapping my legs around the darkness and closing my eyes, gritting my teeth as I held onto the black, oily monster. Grant cried out and I opened my eyes. He was above me, dangling in the air by a foot. The smoke let him go and he dropped to the street.

"Grant!"

He hopped up and shook his head. "I'm fine. Didn't hurt," he quipped as he dove back in, wrapping himself around the heart of the darkness.

I bore down, pushing it into a smaller entity, using my energy to wrap it into a smaller and smaller ball of evil. It pushed tendrils out and Grant was there, pressing them back in, compacting it into itself. When it was the size of a tennis ball, I called out for Tristan to bring the jar. He held it out and Evie tried to guide the smoke in but drew her hand back. Her face crumpled.

"I can't," she said quietly.

Tristan held out the jar and Grant and I moved it into the opening. It wouldn't fit. We shoved again and again.

"We have to make it smaller," I told Grant.

"I don't have anything left," he panted.

Me neither. I closed my eyes and thought of my mom. I had watched her give every last ounce of her strength to fight the cancer growing within her and somehow coming up with a last reserve, a last bubble of strength, every time. I focused on that feeling and felt a spark inside. I pushed it out into my fingertips and the smoke compacted one last time. It shot into the jar and Tristan slammed the lid on the top, holding it there while he lit the wick. The first dribble of wax ran down, covering the lid. Tristan turned it around and around in his hands, coating the outside of the jar with a layer of wax.

"Did we get it?" Grant asked. He was lying on his back in the middle of the street.

I chuckled and sat next to him. "Yeah, we got it."

He smiled up at me. "That was amazing."

"You want out yet?"

He propped himself up on his elbow. "Are you seriously asking me that right now?"

"I figured I haven't asked you for a bit. Thought it was appropriate."

Grant tried to gather me in his arms, but they met no resistance and went right through me.

I swallowed. "I'll be fine."

"We need to go." He nodded toward the group and stood up with a grunt. "You can't last like this."

"I know." I walked over and looked at my friends. They were watching Tristan spinning the jar around, coating it on all sides with the melting wax. It hardened, layer upon layer, until the angry smoke whirling around inside was completely blocked from view.

"We have to go."

Andy looked up. "Come on, guys."

Tristan placed the jar behind an alcove of a building. "We'll get it once we get our bodies back."

Evie walked over to the front of the house and put her foot on the first step. She pressed down and it held. Giving us the thumbs up, she climbed the rest of them with us all close behind. Standing at the door, she turned the handle. It glided open on quiet hinges, revealing the beautiful house beyond. We stepped into the foyer. A huge staircase wrapped up to a balcony and the handrail was adorned with a draping of fresh spring flowers.

"It looks like what Mr. Williams showed us," Evie breathed.

"She's in here," I said, grabbing her hand and pointing to the parlor on our left. We moved into the doorway.

Charlotte paced the floor, tears running down her face as she read the letter from Jacob.

"That letter was written by Lottie. We have to make her see that it's a lie."

I watched as Charlotte crossed to the window, placing her palm to the glass. My heart broke for her. She had lived in this nightmare for over a century.

Grant walked into the room and stood next to Charlotte. He closed his eyes and as he reached out to touch the glass, it wavered. Andy walked in and stood facing the glass, bringing a hand up to rest on Grant's shoulder. Charlotte's expression changed. She stared at the window and tilted her head to the side.

"Jacob?"

Andy passed the memory of Jacob reading her letter in the night through Grant and projected it onto the window's surface.

Charlotte watched, transfixed, as Jacob read her letter, and then proclaimed his love for her and his daughter, Mattie. A hand flew up to her mouth as Jacob was pulled into the darkness of the locket. She blinked several times, as if she was coming out of a trance. Then, she turned to me, her eyes flying open wide as she took in the people standing in her parlor.

"Charlotte, my name is Marissa, and I'm your," I hesitated. "I'm your family. Charlotte, Lottie has been twisting your memories of Jacob. He never stopped loving you, right up to the moment he died. He always loved you. It was always you." I took a step back, letting her process my words.

She shook her head a tic. "But, the letter?" She looked at her empty hands and then up at me, her eyes questioning.

"Lottie wrote the letter. She wanted you to see what she wanted you to see to cause you pain. To keep you trapped because she loved Jacob and he loved you."

Charlotte brought a dainty hand up to her face. "I-I do not understand. Jacob left us, he left us!" Her face crumpled and hid behind her hands.

"Charlotte, Lottie arranged for her father to have him sent on a mission trip to Missouri. She wanted him gone."

"But, why, why did he not come back to us?"

I shook my head. "He couldn't. He was trapped in a town called Culvers Grove and he wanted to get back to you, but he couldn't."

"He's here now," Grant said.

Charlotte looked around wildly.

"Well, not exactly *here*," I said. "We brought him here in a locket. And, Charlotte, Mattie is here, too."

Realization clouded her features and her eyes filled with tears. "Mattie?"

"Yes, they're both here, but we have to get them away from Lottie."

"Mattie?"

Charlotte wandered back to the window and stood looking down into the basinet. She reached out and moved the afghan. Her scream almost shattered my ears.

"Where is she?" she cried. "Where's my baby? She was right here!"

"Shhh," I said. "She's here, but we have to get her to you. She's just outside."

Charlotte nodded and attempted a small smile. "Would you all like some tea? I can have the kitchen staff make some up for you. Oh! Where are my manners? I have not even offered you a snack and you must be so weary from your travels." She began bustling about the room, straightening pillows and running her hands down the skirt of her dress in a repetitive motion.

Grant looked over at me, his eyes wary.

"She's been shown a false memory for a long time," I said. "It's done some damage." I stood close to Charlotte and took her hand away from the table she was straightening. "Charlotte, would you like to see Jacob?"

Her eyes filled with tears. "More than anything in this world."

I nodded and led her over to Evie. "These are my friends, Evie, Andy, and Tristan. They're going to help you get to Jacob."

Andy and Tristan stared at Charlotte.

"Nice to meet you," Tristan said. "Can you show us to the garden?"

She smiled tentatively and nodded. "Yes, um, yes."

As we walked by the staircase, she looked up at it. "So beautiful," she mused.

We crept to the back doors, fanning out to look through the windows located on either side.

I stared out at the garden, the summer sun washing it in buttery light. Flowers adorned every surface. The fountain bubbled with crystal clear water. Beyond the fountain, under twin trees hanging with Spanish moss, Andy, Tristan, and Evie were perched on chairs, their eyes empty and their features slack. Beyond them stood a cloaked figure. Her back was toward us and she was intent on something she was holding. I tried not to look at the figure of my boyfriend slumped on the ground next to her. Taking a deep breath, I turned to Evie and touched her shoulder.

"Can you see the spikes?"

She nodded. "Yeah, she has everyone."

"You all know what to do?"

Andy and Tristan nodded, their eyes never leaving the backyard.

"Charlotte," I said, "I need you to wait right here. When you see Jacob and Mattie, I want you to go to them, but not before you see them. Do you understand?"

Her eyes teared up and she nodded. "I will do as you asked. Tell me again, who did you say you were?"

"I am your great, great, great, great, great granddaughter."

She smiled and reached out to touch my face gently. "You are so beautiful. And, you have his eyes."

I smiled and pressed my hand to hers. Energy sparked between us.

Charlotte recoiled. "My goodness!" She stood looking at her hand.

"It's time," Evie said.

I turned to look at the window. In the garden, Lottie had removed her hood and I saw my hair cascading down her back.

I narrowed my eyes. "Let's go."

CHAPTER 26

We snuck out and left Charlotte standing by the door. Evie, Tristan, Grant, and Andy hid behind the fountain and the bushes that circled it. I crept around the bushes and got as close as possible to the figure. Our spectral feet made no noise upon the ground as we walked. Lottie had moved from the tree and was chanting under her breath a short distance away. Tristan moved his foot against the bushes and the leaves rustled.

Lottie turned toward the back of the house and looked up, her, well my, eyes watchful. As I stared at her, anger grew inside me. It was so soft at first that I barely noticed it, but it grew each moment that I looked at her and before I knew it, I was seething with fury. She had hurt so many people. She had caused so much pain. And, for what? To get back at Charlotte for "stealing" Jacob? She had tried to kill little Mattie and had kept Jacob locked in a town hundreds of miles away from his love. She'd caused spirits to exist in pain for so many years and kept families apart. All because of her all-consuming selfishness.

I was wrong. I'd thought in the cabin she was worthy of pity, but as I stared at her, I knew that she was past retribution. She was pure evil.

After a bit, Lottie dropped her eyes to the object in her hands and began chanting again. The locket began to glow around the edges. Grant's body lay motionless at her feet.

The locket started to vibrate in her hands, sending out flashes of purple and green into the air around her. Her brow furrowed. She stopped chanting and fumbled in the pocket of her cloak. She brought out a jar and placed it on the ground with a glassy sound. Then, she sat on the ground and continued to chant. The locket opened around the edges and the purple shot out through the crack and suddenly Mattie was standing in front of Lottie, her cheeks high with color.

Lottie stared at her for a moment and then a slow smile alit on her face. "Why, Mattie, I did not believe our paths would ever cross again."

I cringed at the sound of the hag's voice coming from my lips.

"I hate you!" Mattie spat. "I've lived in fear for decades, but I'm not afraid of you anymore!" Her hands were balled into fists at her sides.

Lottie smiled and tilted her head at an odd angle. She leaned in toward Mattie and whispered. "And, that, my dear, makes you a very stupid girl." She flicked her wrist and a ball of energy shot out, arcing over Mattie and lifting her into the air.

Mattie's spirit went rigid and her eyes went blank. Lottie flicked her wrist again and Mattie began shaking. A tiny squeak escaped her mouth followed by a thin strand of drool as she shook, her toes dragging on the ground as she moved in the air above.

"Leave her alone!" Charlotte sprang from her spot by the door, jettisoning herself toward Lottie, fury pouring from her essence.

I reached out to stop her, but it was too late.

Lottie looked up with an amused expression. She let the locket fall on the chain to her chest and flicked the wrist of her other hand, catching Charlotte mid-charge in an arc of electricity. "Well, now," she said, raising her voice. "It appears that we have additional guests for this afternoon's ceremony. And, if we have Charlotte, then that means little mice have let her out."

Lottie moved her right hand to her left, Charlotte moving toward Mattie. They arced together and embraced. Lottie held out the jar and brought her hand down to its lip. Mattie and Charlotte poured into the jar, their spirits taffy-like as they stretched in the space. Lottie hummed while she placed the lid on top and lit a candle. It glowed poison green and the wax coated the top. When she was done, she placed the jar on the lip of the fountain. Standing back, she smiled, and then looked up toward the house.

"Now, little mice, where are you?"

I turned to look at Evie. Her mouth was open and she looked more scared than I'd ever seen. Andy, Grant, and Tristan were creeping back toward the doors, but Evie was frozen in place.

"Come out, come out, wherever you are!" Lottie swept her hands back and forth as she approached, bushes flying apart in her wake. I pushed myself back as far as I could into the bush I was hiding behind, watching helplessly as she bore down on my friends.

Lottie swept her hands a final time and the bush in front of my friends exploded, sending twigs and leaves scattering across the ground. Evie, Andy, Grant, and Tristan stood up.

Evie's cheeks grew red and I saw her eyes spark. "You will let them go," she said, the tremor in her voice belying her confidence.

Lottie considered her for a moment. "Now, how did you get out?"

Andy spoke up. "Your jars were made of, well, glass. Pretty easy to break."

"Aren't you a clever little mouse?" Lottie turned for a moment to consider Andy, and then narrowed her eyes at Evie. "Now, who let Charlotte out?"

Evie's jaw jutted out and she remained silent.

Lottie approached, her head swinging side to side in a serpentine manner. Tristan balled up his fists, but Andy held a hand out to his chest and shook his head once. The motion did not go unnoticed by Lottie.

"Let me help you with that," she said, muttering a chant and sweeping a hand out from her cloak. The three boys went rigid, their eyes wide.

Evie cried out. "Leave them alone! It was me! I can see spikes in the fabric. I saw one over this house and I was able to talk to Charlotte."

Lottie was inches from Evie's face. "And where did you get these powers from?"

"From Marissa. She helped me get back into my body when I was in a coma. Some of her must have gotten into me."

"Then, that's a part I want," Lottie said with a flick of her wrist, rendering Evie rigid and silent, "but that can wait until after the ceremony. Come." She moved her hands and my friends floated across the garden to the base of the trees. There, she froze them above where their bodies sat, eyes rolling wildly in their sockets. Bile rose in my throat.

I closed my eyes against the tears and concentrated on Lottie's movements. She stood next to Grant's body and looked down at him, her essence predatory. She slipped out of the cloak and stood there in a white lace wedding dress. The afternoon sun lit it up, but something dark hid under the lace. Then, she brought the locket into her hands again and rubbed a hand over it lovingly.

"My love," she crooned as she stroked the locket. The green light grew around the edges and the locket began to open as she chanted. Her eyes rolled back in her head and the chanting got louder. Suddenly, Jacob's form sprang from the locket and he stood before her, confusion clouding his features.

She rolled her head forward and gazed upon him. "Jacob, my love."

He looked around, his stance defensive. "Who are you?"

"It's our wedding day, my love."

Jacob stared at her and then shook his head. "No. No, I am wed to Charlotte. We-we have a daughter."

"No, my love. Do you not remember? Charlotte died in childbirth and the baby was stillborn. The shock must have been too much." She reached out to touch him, but he drew away from her.

"Who are you?" he said again.

For a moment, my face disappeared behind a shimmering image of Lottie. She was beautiful, dark hair swept up and dark eyes peering out from an alabaster face. She smiled and reached out again. This time, Jacob allowed her to touch him. He blinked several times as she showed him a memory. One I was sure she had fabricated. As the memory ended, Jacob fell to his knees on the ground, his shoulders shaking with sobs.

"Oh, my dearest Charlotte. My little one. No!"

Lottie came around him and put her arm on his shoulders. "My sweet Jacob. I am so sorry to tell you of this great loss. We tried to write while you were in Missouri, but the post was delayed. You came home several weeks ago, but have been inconsolable. It has only been my love that has gotten you through these darkest of times. Do you not remember that you asked me to marry you but a month ago? Oh, dear, you don't remember, do you?" She sat back on her haunches.

Jacob peered up at her from red-rimmed eyes. "I do not remember coming home. Only being somewhere cold. And dark. Oh, Ottolie, it was so very dark where I was."

She reached out and took his hands. "See, Jacob? I helped you when you came back. I helped you to become whole again. Now, let me help you. Let me take care of you and we can finally be together. As it always should have been."

As she spoke, a tendril of black smoke rose from her wrist and snaked out, wrapping around Jacob, caressing his face and tightening around his wrists and ankles. As a wisp came up to his face, it poised above his ear, almost seeming to wait for further instructions. Lottie nodded her head and the smoke filtered into his ear. When it did, his eyes went blank.

"There, now, my love. It is time to complete the ceremony. We will be together forever after now. Come?" She stood up and offered her hand to him.

Jacob blinked, the smoke overtaking his face. He took her hand and used it to stand. He looked like a broken man, his shoulders slumped and all of the light gone from his eyes.

Lottie led him to Grant's body. "Now, my love, I need you to step into this, well, this suit of clothes. For the wedding." She placed a hand on his shoulder.

I wondered what images she was showing him. Pressing my lips together, I crouched, ready to pounce. The time was near. I held out my hand and looked through it to the ground below. I wasn't going to last much longer. She was getting stronger and I was fading away. I closed my eyes and shook my head, trying to clear it.

When I opened then, Lottie's head rolled back on her shoulders, her eyes closed as she chanted louder and louder.

That's when I pounced.

I hit Lottie hard. Enough to knock her back and off her feet. Her eyes flew open and then darkened with recognition.

"You!" she screamed, grabbing at handfuls of my hair.

I fought back, tearing at the lace neckline of her dress. I could see a glowing ember below. *That's mine!* I grabbed at it as her fingernails raked across my face. The pain was astronomical and I cried out, the burning along my cheek white hot. I clawed at the glowing ember, but wasn't able to get my fingers around it with Lottie writhing beneath me. She brought up a hand and clouted me on the side of the head. I saw dots of light and almost threw up. Shaking my head, I was met with her other hand as it came up and landed squarely on my nose. I heard a crunch and blood poured into my mouth.

"Stop it!"

"Get off her!"

"Leave her alone!"

My friends' voices floated into my consciousness but so focused was I on the glowing ember that their voices fell into part of the background. Lottie bit down on my arm and I screamed, hitting at her face with the butt of my hand. I felt something give underneath her skin. Her head lolled to the side and then froze.

In that moment of clarity, I focused my attention on Lottie's chest. I saw the glowing ember, red and full of life. I reached out for the ember, my fingers finally closing around it. As they did, my soul was sucked into something, a vortex, and I began spinning in the darkness.

The portal spit me out on the wet ground and I sat up, looking around for danger. I was back on the island, but this time, I wasn't alone.

CHAPTER 27

Standing with her back to me was a girl. She was clad in a pink dress that had a high neck and lace along the bodice. Her back was ramrod straight and her feet were bare. She stood staring out at the lake that surrounded the island.

I stood rooted to the spot for one minute, two, maybe a million minutes. Time meant nothing here. It was only the girl, the moon, and me. The water lapped at the shores. Rhythmic. Repetitive. The sound quieted my soul. I reached down and felt my chest. Within it, was a warm ember, spreading its warmth through me, filling me and making me whole again. I considered the girl and began to walk toward her. When I was close enough, I put out my hand and rested it on her shoulder.

The girl turned her head. Her profile was dainty, proud, her upturned nose giving her an aloof look. "It was never meant to go this far," she said, her voice echoing around me on the island.

"Lottie?" I whispered.

She turned then and stared at me. We were about the same height and she looked to be around my age. Her features were dark, but not menacing. This was Lottie before she became twisted and angry. This was Lottie before the dark magic took hold of her with its teeth.

"I only wanted my mother," she said. A single tear ran along her cheek and she turned to walk to the water's edge. She crouched down, the hem of her dress getting wet. I followed her and stood next to her as she touched the surface. The water rippled out from her touch, lit on the edges by the moonlight. Within the circles, an image grew.

A small version of Lottie stood at a bedside. A woman lay upon the bed, her frail frame ravaged by sickness. She held out a hand to Lottie and the girl took it, holding onto it while she cried.

I bit my bottom lip as I watched to keep it from trembling.

"Lottie, I'm so sorry that happened to your mother. It happened to mine, too."

She peered out over the water, and then touched it again. The ripples spread and within this image was that of a ship cutting its way across the ocean. Standing near the bow was the small version of Lottie. She stood on a box to see over the edge and the wind whipped her hair around her face. A man walked up behind her.

"My little princess, this is quite an adventure we are on."

"That was my father. He moved me away from my mother when she died. To a new place. A place I did not know."

"My dad did that, too," I said, crouching next to her.

Lottie reached out to touch the water again, but this time, she grabbed a handful of sand. She stood up in a fluid motion and threw the sand. It landed in the water, sending out a cacophony of ripples. Within each, one of my awful memories began to play. Each one playing a time I was unable to help a ghost in Culvers Grove. I stared at them, my throat working as I tried to swallow.

I wasn't looking at her when she lunged at me. She was upon me, biting and scratching, grabbing at the ember within my chest. I pushed her away but she kept coming at me, over and over again. I fell onto the shore, the sand scratching at my back as Lottie put her hands around my throat. She pressed down with all of her power, shutting off my windpipe and pressing my head under the water. I grappled at her hands with mine, but I couldn't pull them off. Her eyes were dark pools of hate, wavering through the layer of water over my face. Her teeth were gritted in a wide smile as she held my throat, killing me. My hands lost all feeling and fell to my sides. I was helpless. My vision began to cloud around the edges and I opened and closed my mouth, trying to suck air into my burning lungs, the gritty water coating my tongue.

The water began to boil behind me and I rolled my eyes to see something coming up through the water toward us. Lottie's eyes opened wide and she let go of me, backpedaling on her rear end on the shore. I dragged myself from the water, my hair clinging to my face as I gulped lungfuls of the sweet night air. My throat was on fire.

"Marissa!"

The voice came from behind me and I whipped around to see Grant's hand reaching from the surface.

Grant held his palm to the reflection of the water and I could see Evie, Tristan, and Andy there as well.

The images on the surface of the water had changed from ones I recognized to unfamiliar ones. People crying, souls dying, death and rot. Sadness filled me as I realized that these were Lottie's memories. *Her* darkness.

"Hey, my paranormal princess," Grant said.

A choked sob escaped my lips and I reached out for him. As we made contact, he began pulling me toward him. I looked back at Lottie. As I watched, the façade of youth began to fade and she turned twisted and gnarled, darkness incarnate as we drifted away. Grant pulled at me and I turned toward him.

"It's going to be okay," I whispered.

A moment before the portal closed around us, I could feel something ripping, tearing from my core. I looked down, horror filling me as I watched a tendril of smoke rip the glowing ember from my chest. The pain was instant and intense. I screamed and made a grab at it with my free hand. The smoke yanked it away, across the dark waters, toward the island. Into Lottie's gnarled hands.

You have no choice now. I have what made you special. I have what I need.

Her voice filled my head, banging against my skull and leaving slick oily thoughts where it touched.

You're mine now, Marisssaaaaa.

A scream full of hate echoed from her mouth, filling the space around the island. I fell into Grant's arms and rocketed into the darkness with him until we came out on the other side.

CHAPTER 28

I landed on the ground and looked up. The sun shone on me, filtering through the Spanish moss-covered limbs. Clouds streamed through the blue sky. I knew that people moved around me, and there were voices. I let the warmth spread through me and closed my eyes again. I felt complete and without pain for the first time in days and I didn't want it to end. The warmth spread to my core.

A moment later, though, the pain came.

Yet, it was different this time. This time, it wasn't the burning I was familiar with or the pressure on my chest that had haunted me since we left Culvers

Grove. No, this pain came with a feeling of emptiness. Of something missing. I looked down at my chest. The collar of my shirt had been ripped, and beneath, the hole was there. I held my hand out and saw right through it to the tree limbs above me. I was fading away. I had to get into my body or I would fade away altogether, just as Evie had almost done in her hospital bed.

But how will you get back into your body if you can't walk between the worlds anymore?

"St. Louis?" Evie stood a few feet from me, her curly hair framing her face as the sun created a buttery halo around her hair. She was looking in my direction, but her eyes weren't focused.

"I'm here. I'm fine." *No, I'm not.*

"Oh, St. Louis," she breathed, tears immediately making her eyes glassy. "We have to get you back into your body."

Her understanding about broke me. I took a shaky breath and nodded. It was all I could do not to fall to pieces. *How am I going to tell her that I can't?*

"Come on," she said, motioning to a spot near the giant elm. "It's over here."

I took a deep breath and passed Jacob, who was spinning around slowly, his toes dragging along the ground as the smoke held him like a fly in a spiderweb. I felt bile rise in my throat and gave him a silent apology as I passed. I couldn't help him now. I wasn't going to be able to help anyone anymore.

Andy, Tristan, and Grant stood in a circle in the shade of the enormous elm, staring at something by their feet. I followed Evie over and then looked down, too, my hand flying over my mouth when I saw it.

My body lay on the ground, twisted and dark. It writhed around, the eyes rolled back in its head. The ember in my body's chest glowed black, spreading a tarlike substance through the veins. The hair was matted to the side of my head and a trickle of blood ran from the corner of my mouth.

"Is she in there?" Grant said.

The pain I heard in his voice physically hurt me. I reached out and touched his shoulder.

He drew in a ragged breath and spun around. "Marissa?"

"I'm here," I said.

Tears filled his eyes. He tried to hug me, but his hands went right through me. I could feel the anguish rising off him in waves.

"Anderson, we have to get her out of your body."

Tristan nodded. "She's killing you."

Lottie was killing it from the inside out, and if we waited much longer, there wouldn't be any body left to which I could return. *Even if you could.*

I took a deep breath. "We have to get the ember from my body's chest and trap it in the locket. Lottie's soul is connected to it. If we can get the ember, we can get her."

"There's something she's not telling us." Evie peered at me. "You're hiding something."

My eyes filled with tears and I sat hard on the ground. My fingers had nearly disappeared. I folded my arms, hiding my hands under my elbows. I took a deep breath. "We have to work quickly. Tristan, get the locket and hold it open toward the sun. Grant, you will have to reach through the reflection the sun makes on the glass. Evie, you can direct him to where the ember is. Do you see it?"

She nodded. "I can see the colors around it." Her lip curled a bit with disgust as she looked at the ember.

"Andy? I need you to help Tristan hold onto the locket once she's inside. Keep it closed. Then, get it back to the cabin. You know how to trap it, right?"

He nodded.

Evie stared at me and raised an eyebrow.

"We have to trap her. She can't hurt anyone else," I whispered. "Worry about me later."

She stared at me a moment longer and then nodded, her chin trembling. "Come on. Let's do this."

Tristan walked over to where the locket had fallen to the ground. He concentrated intently on it and was able to finally grab it and carry it over to us. My body convulsed on the ground and began to foam at the mouth. I looked away.

"Hold it like that. Grant, can you see the reflection?"

"Yeah. Don't move it. Keep it steady."

"It's right here in her chest."

"I can't see that."

I opened my eyes and saw my friends bent over my body. Grant reached through the locket, squinting as he searched.

"I can only see darkness."

"Here," Evie said. She reached in with Grant and guided his hand. "There it is."

My body bucked once, twice and then lay quiet. My foot twitched and my head fell to the side.

"Hold onto it," Evie said, drawing her hand back. "Get ready, Tristan."

Grant's arm was yanked further into the locket and he cried out. Then, he set his jaw and pulled, the tendons standing out on his arm. He drew her spirit from the surface of the glass and for a moment, he held it in his hand, the dark ember pulsating like a heartbeat.

I stared at it, transfixed. It was Lottie's darkness, but it was also part of me. Part of me that I never thought I wanted, but a part of me that had turned out to mean everything. Tears slid down my face as Tristan clamped the locket closed and slid the clasp. He muttered the binding spell he'd found and the locket stopped moving, lying dormant in the palm of his hand.

He looked up at Andy. "That's it," he said, a slow smile spreading on his face. "We got her!"

As soon as he quit concentrating on it, the locket slid through his spectral hand and landed on the ground at my feet. I considered it as it lay gleaming in the afternoon sun. This object that had caused so much pain and now contained the soul of the person that had caused all of that hurt. My friends would take the locket to the cabin and make sure it could no longer hurt anyone else.

But, then, we'll all fade away.

I looked up at my friends' spirits, high fiving and laughing. My insides broke apart. I looked down, expecting to see my spirit broken into shards. The pain I felt now was like none I had ever felt before. I had dragged them all into this and now, they would never return home. They wouldn't get to say goodbye to their families. Their moms would never be able to hug them again. They wouldn't get to go to school, dances, or graduation. They'd followed me into the fire, and now we were all getting burned.

"I'm sorry," I whispered between sobs. "I'm so sorry."

Evie stopped and turned her head to me. "Guys, stop. St. Louis, what's wrong?" She knelt beside me.

Andy, Tristan, and Grant were immediately by my side.

Grant reached out and touched my face. His hand slid through completely. He blinked and then recovered. He held out his hand. "Come on, babe, let's get you back in your body."

I smiled a sad smile and shook my head. "Lottie has part of me. Before you pulled me out of the island, she took the part that let me walk between the worlds. It's gone and now..."

"And, without it, you can't get back into your body," Grant finished, taking his hand back and standing up. His features were strained and his mouth was drawn into a thin line.

I shook my head.

"There has to be another way," Tristan said. He furrowed his brow and started pacing. "What if Grant reaches through and pulls you back into your body? He can open a portal and, and..." he stopped and looked around. "We have to find a mirror."

"It doesn't work that way," Grant said quietly.

Tristan stopped for a second. "Well, we have to get her back to the cabin. Lottie was able to take over bodies all of these years. She must have known how to take over a body, right? There has to be a spell there."

"That's it!" I said, everything snapping into focus. "Go to the cabin. Find the spell she used to get back into your bodies."

"It's only a bandage, though, St. Louis. Why do you think she needed you so badly? She was able to use a body for her soul, but it was never truly hers. She wasn't bound to it. It was only a vessel."

"But, it's better than the alternative," I said, my voice small. "Go, please? Before it's too late for you all. I'll be fine. I'll wait here for you to get back."

Evie shook her head. "You won't be here by the time we get back, St. Louis. You won't even be here in five minutes." Her nostrils flared as she looked down.

Tristan gasped.

My feet had completely faded and my legs were gone beneath my knees.

"It's fine," I said, crying. "I'm fine."

"What are you hiding?" Evie narrowed her eyes and pulled down my shirt collar, revealing the gaping hole in my chest. She stared at it. "Is that...?"

I closed my eyes. "It was the part of me that made me special," I said quietly.

Andy barked with laughter.

My head snapped up.

"Are you kidding me?" he asked. "You think that *that's* what made you special?"

"You, Marissa Anderson, are the kindest person I've ever met." Tristan stepped forward and knelt next to me. He looked into my eyes as he took my hand. "You were my friend and you never judged me."

Andy knelt and took the hand that Tristan was holding. "You're the most giving person I know. You think about everyone else before you think about yourself. You're smart and wicked funny, you know, even when you're not trying." He smiled.

Evie took my other hand. "You and your dad are my *family*, St. Louis. I can't imagine my life if you hadn't come to Culvers Grove."

Grant sniffed and wiped at his eyes with the back of his hand. He knelt then and gently cupped my face with his hands. His touch was a whisper. He looked into my eyes, his gaze unwavering. "I love you with every single bit of my being, Marissa. You are my everything."

"I'm sorry," I said. "I'm so sorry to all of you. Please tell my dad I love him so much." I couldn't hardly talk around the sobs. "I love all of you."

Evie looked over at Andy. He nodded.

"St. Louis, I'm giving you my power back. What I took from you when you put me back into my body."

I shook my head. "No, you need it."

She smiled. "You need it more."

Electricity sparked on my hand and I looked down. Green light arced, passing from her hand into mine.

"Me, too, Anderson. It's not fair to the rest of the world that I'm this handsome *and* have supernatural powers."

"Yeah, I'm giving back what I took," Tristan said. "Sorry about that, by the way."

Red and light blue spread into my right hand, from theirs to mine.

Grant smiled and closed his eyes, his light passing from him into me. The lights swirled into my spirit, racing along my arms up to my chest where they spun into a ball, filling up the hole.

"It's a rainbow," Evie whispered. "I always knew it was."

CHAPTER 29

Andy stood up first, holding out his hand to me. I grabbed it and stood up, my spirit buzzing with energy and strength. Everyone else followed me over to where my body lay on the ground, still. So still. I stared down at it.

Here goes nothing. I looked over at Andy for any sign that he'd heard me. He stared at the ground.

I looked back at my friends. "Thank you," I whispered and then reached out for my body. I grabbed hold of my wrist and sent myself shooting down and into it. I spiraled for a moment as my soul settled into my body. Then, I opened my eyes.

The sun filtered through the leaves and the sunlight was about the most beautiful thing I'd ever seen. I sat up, coughing and sputtering. Wiping away the blood and spittle from the corner of my mouth with the back of my hand, I looked around. Panic pricked at my consciousness. Where were they?

I turned my head this way and that. I was in the garden and I was alone.

"Evie! Grant!" I scrambled to my feet, my muscles crying out in protest. "Andy! Tristan!"

I bit my bottom lip and focused on the spot where I left my friends. First, I saw colors, and then a figure appeared. It was only an outline, but then it snapped into focus.

"Hey, Anderson."

Other figures appeared from the sides and then I could see them all again. I let the panic rise up from my throat and it came out a laugh. My laughter filled the garden as I looked at my friends. "It worked! It worked!"

"How about getting us all back in our bodies now, St. Louis?"

"Oh, my gosh, yes! Evie come here." I stood next to her body and swiped at the black smoke holding it down to the chair. The smoke dissipated with the motion and I reached out for her hand. She passed through me and into her body, her soul feeling familiar as it ran through my mine.

Evie sat up and blinked. She ran her hands through her hair, pulling it away from her face. Then, she put her palms on her arms, chest, and legs. "I'm here," she said, looking up at me. "I'm all here!"

"Me next, me next," Andy said, hopping up and down next to me.

I wiped the smoke away from his body and then allowed him to pass through me to it. His eyes opened and he sat up. "I need to get some food. My body's starving!"

I helped Tristan and Grant back into their bodies. Tristan and Andy wrapped one another in a hug.

"Now, let's try this again," Grant said, stepping close. He enveloped me in his arms and leaned down to kiss me. His lips pressed into mine, warm and safe. It felt like home.

When he drew away, I looked up at him. "I love you, too, you know. For so many reasons."

He winked. "You can tell me all about them on the drive home."

"We need to let Jacob and Charlotte and Mattie go," I said. "They deserve to be together after all this time."

I walked over to where Jacob spun above the ground. I knocked away the smoke and it released him with a hiss before disappearing into the air. He fell to the ground and lay there, his eyes staring straight ahead.

"Is everything okay?" Evie asked.

"I don't know." I knelt next to him. "Jacob?"

He blinked and looked up at me. "I...know...you," he said. His eyes narrowed. "You were in the cavern."

I nodded. "I'm your family, Jacob. Your great great great great great granddaughter, Marissa."

He sat up and shook his head. "No. Charlotte died, and Mattie," he drew a sharp breath in, "she died, too."

"No, Jacob. Lottie told you those things but they weren't true. She wanted you to forget about Charlotte so you would marry her. Charlotte spent the rest of her life waiting for you and Mattie lived a long time as well. She had a son. And he had a son. And so on until me."

"I do not understand." He shook his head.

"Lottie was in love with you. She wanted to marry you but you fell in love with Charlotte instead. When you did, she was so angry that she decided that if she couldn't have you, no one could. So, she learned black magic and then cursed the locket she gave to you as a wedding present. It killed you and then kept killing others. You were trapped in Culvers Grove, um, the town where you died, and Lottie kept your soul trapped there so you couldn't ever return to Savannah to be with Charlotte."

He stared at me, his eyes darkening. "*Lottie* did this thing?"

I nodded. "After you died, she told Charlotte that you left her and found someone else." I hesitated. This next part would be difficult for him to hear. "Lottie tried to kill Mattie. She tried to drown her, but Mr. Williams saved her. When he saved her, she was almost gone. One foot in this world and one in the other."

"The other?"

"Where you are now. It's like a layer overlaying our world."

He squinted at me. "Then how are you able to see me and speak with me."

"When Mattie almost died, she gained the power to walk between those two worlds. She passed the power down to her son, and he to his son, and so on and so on until there's, well, there's me."

"Lottie sent me away and then tried to *kill* my daughter? She kept me from my family? For years and years? What kind of a monster is she?" A darkness took over his features and he began to pace, smoke beginning to swirl around his feet.

"Stop," I said gently. "Take a deep breath, Jacob. We have trapped Lottie in the locket and we're going to make sure that she never hurts another living soul. Or, dead ones either for that matter." I looked at the smoke swirling around his ankles. "Please stop. I have Charlotte and Mattie here."

He stopped and the darkness dropped. He stared at me. "Charlotte? She's alive?"

I dropped my gaze. "Not anymore, Jacob. She's a ghost, like you, but she's here. So is Mattie. Do you want to see them?"

His eyes filled with tears. "Charlotte? My love is here?"

I nodded and walked over and took the jar from the fountain's edge. I used a rock to crack away at the wax. Finally, I got it all chipped off and then used my shirt to gain a grip on the lid. I twisted and Charlotte and Mattie's spirits shot out. They landed on the ground and took form.

Mattie faced her father. "Hello, Father."

Jacob stared at her. "Mattie? My little one?" He strode over and held her in a gentle embrace, pressing his cheek to the top of her head. Her arms wrapped around his middle and she held onto him, crying and laughing.

He held her at arm's length, staring down into her face. "I thought you were gone forever. I-I remember seeing you before, not so long ago. You stood before me and then it was all darkness for so long."

"I ran away from Savannah when I was sixteen, after Mother died. It wasn't safe for me to be here."

"Lottie?" Jacob's voice had a hard edge to it.

"Yes, Lottie. She gave me no peace while I lived here and I was in fear for my life. So, I left under the guise of being a young man looking to ride for the pony express. I left on a stage bound for St. Joseph, Missouri." She looked up at her father. "I never made it that far, though. The stage was taken down by a tribe of natives and I barely escaped with my life. Everyone on the coach was killed. I lay in a riverbed for three days' time, an arrow encased in my side. Finally, a man rode by. His name was Charles Scott and he was the son of a wealthy landowner in Culvers Grove. He took me in and nursed me back to health. He found that I was a woman in disguise and agreed to keep up my ruse. We didn't mean to fall in love, but we did and when I found that I was with child, he had a cabin built in the forest on the edge of his family's land. I had a son, Henry, and Charles allowed us to live there, regularly giving us money and providing food. It was a very good life, Father, but for the fear of being discovered by Lottie. I lived the rest of my life in disguise, only allowing Henry and Charles to know the truth."

Jacob held her to him. "My poor dear daughter. I am so sorry I was not able to protect you."

I took a step forward. "Mattie ended up in the same town where you died, Jacob, but she had no idea your spirit was there. You had turned into something very dark and very dangerous."

Jacob looked up at me. "The loss of everything you love can turn you into something you do not even recognize yourself."

Charlotte stood to the side, her eyes watchful. I walked over to her. "Charlotte, I brought Jacob to you." She took her eyes off him for a moment to look at me. Her features softened and she reached out a hand to touch my face. "I know you. You helped me. And, you brought my love back to me." Her hand fell as Jacob approached, his eyes taking her in.

"My sweet Charlotte."

"My...Jacob."

They stood facing each other, the space between them filled with years of not knowing, lies, and uncertainty. The darkness swirled between them for a moment.

Then, Charlotte tilted her head to the side. "Jacob," she smiled, "you've come back to me."

He smiled and the darkness broke into shards as he stepped forward and gathered her in his arms. He kissed her and they spun around, light shooting out from them.

Jacob looked over his shoulder at Mattie. "Please come with us?"

Mattie smiled, her pretty features lighting up. Then, she turned to me. "Tell Henry that I love him and I'll see him soon?"

I nodded and took her hands. "Bye, Mattie."

She smiled, then turned toward her mother and father and floated up to them. They wrapped their arms around each other. A light so bright I had to look away coated the sky and then, they were gone.

The sunshine faded away and the sounds of the garden muted. I looked over to my group of friends. They were standing in an abandoned building, piles of wood and trash heaped around them. Dust filtered from the ceiling. It was dark outside, but the streetlights shining through the dusty windows offered enough light that I could make my way back to them.

"They're gone, aren't they?" Evie asked.

I nodded. "Yeah. They're gone. So is the house."

"The locket's here," Andy said, nudging it with his toe.

I pressed my lips together. "I guess there's only one thing left to do." Taking a deep breath, I bent and wrapped my fingers around the locket. Darkness and blackness coated it and I shuddered as I dropped the chain around my neck. The locket fell to my chest with a thump and felt like a block of concrete hanging there.

Marisssaaaaa...

"Let's go," I said. "It's time for this to be over once and for all."

CHAPTER 30

After stopping to retrieve the jar of smoke, we made our trek back through the streets of Savannah as everyone was waking up from the night's slumber. A thick frost hung on every blade of grass, and as the sun rose, the frost glittered. It was quite beautiful and I would have to enjoy it...later. Cars roared to life and passed us slowly as tired people sipped on coffee and tuned their radios to the morning shows. The city was alive again and I felt like a traitor as I walked along the sidewalks, holding a hand over the thing of evil hanging from my neck.

We crossed under the highway again and made our way into the forest on the other side. I remembered Mr. Williams' directions and wound my way through the thick underbrush. The train tracks were in front of us and we turned three times to the left and then to the right. The ancient tree appeared along with the small cabin clinging to its root system. I stepped forward but Evie stopped me.

"It didn't work," she said.

"What do you mean?"

"I don't see the tree or the cabin."

I offered my arm.

"Oh."

"Come on."

Everyone followed me as I found the door and opened it.

"Whoa, that was cool, Anderson. It's like it appeared out of nowhere."

"I don't think us regular people can see the entrance," Evie said, stepping through the door.

"That's what I'm counting on," I mumbled. "No one is ever going to find her."

We grabbed the key from the mantle, unlocked the door to the room behind the fireplace, and stood staring at the glass enclosure.

"I hate her," Andy said, his jaw working. "Let's get this thing off."

It took all of us holding onto an edge to get the gigantic glass lid off, but it began to move easily once we broke the edge from the table. We lifted it up and over and placed it carefully on the floor next to the table.

"What now?" Evie breathed.

Before I could answer, mists started to jettison out of windows and doors. They were white and lit from within.

"Can you guys see this?" I whispered.

Evie grabbed my hand and then we all held hands. The room grew silent for a moment as we watched and then a sound rose up around us. At first, I thought it was wailing, like Mary at the bridge. My insides clenched. Then, I realized that it wasn't crying, but laughter. Laughter and talking, souls finding one another. The feeling of love permeated my being and I felt tears running down my face.

When the last soul left, the lights in the model of the town went out and the model was empty.

"The curse is gone now," I said. "I need you all to gather dirt, water, and herbs. We need to clean off the table." I started to run a hand over the model, but Andy grabbed it.

"This one's mine, Anderson." He took his arm and swept the model across the table, wiping it clean with one motion. The model fell from the table, breaking into innocuous bits of wood on the floor. He smiled. "Yeah, I needed that."

Everyone gathered things and brought them to me. I busied myself building a replica of the island on the tabletop.

"Whoa," Evie breathed. "What is that place?" She wrapped her arms across her chest.

"It's a place where you're alone. Forever."

She nodded. "Here," she handed me a sprig of herbs.

I placed them along the shoreline and put the jar of smoke near the edge. Once the island was done, I took the chain of the locket from around my neck and held it in my hand.

My friends stood around me as I placed the locket in the center of the island.

"Ready?" Evie asked.

"Almost." I tilted a pitcher and let clear water surround the island I'd made. Then I touched a fingertip to it. Ripples spread out and images began to play on the surface of the water. "I hope one day you'll be able to see some good within these, Lottie," I said. Then, I nodded at the group. "It's time."

We lifted the glass dome and placed it on the table over the model of the island. The edges crackled on the sand and then met with the table with a solid sound.

"Tristan?"

He nodded and laid the book on the floor near the table. He stared at it for a few minutes and then placed his hands palm down on the glass. He closed his eyes and began to chant. The room filled with his words and the glass pressed into the wood, creating a circle of new wood as it crushed the old wood on top. The glass shuddered and then stood still, a physical barrier between the evil contained within and the world around. Dust covered the glass and I caught one last glimpse of the locket as the dust hid it from view.

Andy nodded once and looked over at us. "It's done."

I didn't know whether to laugh or cry as a million emotions slid through me, making my knees weak. Grant was beside me then, holding me against him and offering the strength I didn't have in that moment.

We walked out the doorway and Tristan locked it behind us. He placed the key reverently on the mantle. We stood in a line, shoulder to shoulder, staring at the shelves upon shelves of jars and earthen pots.

"We need to let them go, too," I whispered.

Grant brought my hand to his lips and kissed it. "We do."

Evie was already beside a shelf, pulling jars out and throwing them at the ground at her feet. Grant and I followed suit. Jars exploded around us. They shattered, the mists inside rising up. Some flitted around us, touching us with gossamer strands before fading away, as if they were saying "thank you." Then Tristan and Andy were there, all throwing jars at the floor.

Soon, the floor was littered with glass and the shelves were empty. Our group stood in the middle, panting and smiling. The cabin seemed lighter somehow, joyful. I led the way out and closed the door behind me. As soon as I closed the door, Tristan gasped.

"It's gone."

"Good," I said. I grabbed Evie's hand and squeezed it. "Time to go home?"

"Time to go home, St. Louis."

CHAPTER 31

After a short trip back to the hotel room to run through the shower and gather our things before checking out, we were back on the road again. Andy had grabbed about a dozen muffins and cereal containers from the breakfast area and doled them out to us when we got into Grant's car. The morning sun shone in our rearview mirrors as we left Savannah. We munched in silence and I checked my messages as we headed across the bridge.

A few were from my dad. They didn't make much sense and I swallowed a bite of blueberry muffin around the lump in my throat.

Grant looked over at me. "What's up?"

I nodded. "Worried about my dad."

He placed his hand palm up on his gearshift and I let mine fall into it. Our fingertips intertwined and he brought my hand to his lips.

It would take a good solid twelve hours of driving before we hit St. Louis, with another four to go before we made it to Culvers Grove. We slept and drove in shifts, all of us exhausted from the night before. When we crossed the Mississippi River into St. Louis, everyone woke up and stared out the windows. The city was lit up, and it was a welcome sight after driving through the lonely country of northern Tennessee and Illinois. We stopped in Wentzville for gas and some food and then headed out again, Grant at the wheel, his headlights cutting the darkness as we drove through farmland.

I smiled, remembering the same drive I'd taken with my dad a few short months before. I glanced behind me at the three sleeping forms who were snoring in tandem. My *friends*. I looked over at Grant and smiled.

He caught me looking and raised his eyebrow. "What's up?" His smile was illuminated by the dashboard lights.

"I was just thinking how different things could have turned out for me."

"What do you mean?"

I took a deep breath. "I mean, Lottie and I were on the same path. She lost her mother. Her dad moved her to a different place and she had to leave everything she knew behind. She was lonely and scared. And angry. I could have turned out like her." I chewed on my thumbnail.

Grant smiled again. "You're not like her, though. You made different choices. Your life path is not determined by the events around you but the choices you make."

"Pretty deep, there, man." Andy yawned from the backseat.

I smiled and took the hand that Grant offered. I looked out the window and I must have drifted off, because my eyes flew open as I felt the car slow and turn. We were at the farm.

"Hey," I grunted, stretching as best I could in the seat.

Grant stared through the windshield. "Hey," he said absently. "Didn't we turn off all the lights when we left?"

I felt the seat pull behind me as Andy leveraged himself up to look. "Yeah, we did."

The house stood quiet in the night, the snow around it reflecting the moonlight. Warm orange light poured from every window.

"Maybe someone came by and turned them on?" I offered. Pinpricks of energy pushed at me as we drove around the side of the house to the back.

"Your dad's car is here," Grant said as his headlights splashed across the back of Dad's car parked next to mine.

I took a deep breath to quell my nerves and I threw open the door as soon as the car stopped. Everyone piled out of the car behind me and we stood looking at the house.

"He's here," I said, turning to Evie. Hope spread through me.

She placed a hand on my arm. "You have to be prepared for him not to be himself, St. Louis. Remember how he was when we left? We've only been gone a few days."

I swallowed. "I know." My eyes burned with tears.

A figure moved to the window, silhouetted against the kitchen light.

"Dad!" I shouted, running up the steps and throwing open the back door.

My dad stood in the kitchen, facing the coffee machine. He was pouring a cup of coffee.

My chin trembled. "Dad?" I said in a small voice.

He put the pot down and turned to look at me. A smile spread out on his face. "Hey, Peanut." He took a sip from his cup and placed it on the counter.

"Unauthorized trip across state lines? What is that, three weeks of grounding?"

I stood for a moment, my feet glued to the linoleum. Then, I ran to him and threw my arms around his neck. My tears came quick and fast as they fell on his flannel shirt.

"Shhh," he said, brushing a hand on my head, smoothing my hair. "It's okay. I'm fine."

I looked up at him. "You were so lost when I left. I didn't know if you would find your way back."

"I'll always find my way back to you, Peanut."

I started crying all over again and then started hiccupping.

"Genevieve," Dad said and held out his arm, gathering her into a hug and kissing us both on top of our heads. "I missed you both so much."

When I finally calmed down enough to stop crying, Dad held me at arm's length. "We need to talk. I sent a text to your parents to let them know you're staying here tonight," he nodded at Andy and Tristan. "And, I believe your parents think you are at college?" he raised an eyebrow at Grant.

"Yes, sir."

"We have some things to address," Dad said.

I shook my head. "How did you know where we were? What happened here? How are you back to normal?"

Dad smiled. "Let's go talk to everyone at once."

"Everyone?"

Dad led me into the dining room. There, at the table was my family. Henry, George, Alice, Sam, Sarah, and Grandma.

"Hey, there. It's about time." Grandma stood up and gave me a hug. "That boyfriend of yours needs to find out where his gas pedal is."

CHAPTER 32

Dad perched on a chair at the head of the table. Grant sat next to me and held out his hand. I took it.

"Can you see them, now?" I asked.

He smiled. "I could see them before. We all can."

I looked over at Evie and she nodded her head.

"How?"

"I've got a few tricks up my sleeve," Grandma said. "Remember Sarah's house?"

"You asked how I got here and how I'm back to normal." Dad smiled. "Well, as normal as I ever was anyway. After the first few nights at Melanie's, Thomas and I got to talking. We got a lot worked out and then, last night, I was talking to him and he looked up and said, 'It's time to go.' He said to tell his mom that he loved her and then he and his dad went flying up into the light. It was the most amazing thing I'd ever seen. When he left, it was as if the world snapped into focus. All the vestiges of the dream state I'd been existing in fell away and I was...*awake.* I told Melanie that everything was going to be fine now and told her it was time for me to go home."

I looked over at Andy. "That was when we let all the spirits go from the model."

He nodded.

"I got here and walked in the back door, looking for you. Melanie said you had gone with your friends to fix something, but didn't know when you'd be back." He took a sip of coffee. "Now, I was prepared to skin your hide for leaving without telling me where you were going, but when I got here, Mom sat me down and she and the family told me about what had been happening in Culvers Grove." His features softened and he reached out, placed his hand on mine, and patted it. "Peanut, I had no idea how bad things were."

"Why didn't you call?" My voice was small. "Why didn't you tell me you were better?"

He shook his head. "Your grandmother knew where you were and that by the time you released all the spirits, you all were alive and well."

"I was keeping an eye on you," she said.

"Now, I have cleaned this house from top to bottom and all of my files are organized and labeled, because I was like a cat on a hot tin roof waiting for you to come home, but I knew you were fine. You all take care of each other." He nodded at my friends.

"Are all the spirits gone?" I asked.

"As far as we can tell, there are a few hanging around waiting for someone or helping to finish up some things, but Culvers Grove is like any other town now," George said. "We were waiting to say 'goodbye' to you, but I think we'll be moving along presently."

I reeled. "They're all gone?"

"Nearly all," Grandma said. "Mary, Theodore, Amalie and her brother. You helped everyone you set out to help."

I took a deep breath.

"You helped me, too, Peanut. I spent so many years denying who I was and what I could do. That's over now. I'm embracing it." Dad took another sip of coffee. "Look, I'm learning. I'm growing." He waggled his eyebrows at me.

"This is...too much," I said. "I mean, I don't know what to say."

"Tell us everything that happened in Savannah," Henry said, his eyes intense.

I cleared my throat. "Well, we arrived…" I told them everything that happened, my friends interjecting and adding to the story as we went along. Dad filled and emptied his coffee cup twice and the sun was beginning to come up by the time we finished.

"Wow," Grandma breathed. "I knew you all were dealing with some heavy stuff, but I had no idea."

Dad sat back in his chair, the wood creaking as he did so. He regarded me for quite a while. "You remind me so much of your mother sometimes." His voice caught. Then, he cleared his throat. "I'm awfully proud to be your dad."

"Well, it's time for us to go," Henry said, standing up from his chair. "George? Alice?"

They nodded and stood as well.

"It was one of my great joys to have met you, Marissa," Alice said, touching my face. "Thank you for all you have done. I'm glad to know you."

"Your mother said she'll see you soon, Henry," I said. "She loves you."

He smiled. "Thank you. Goodbye, Marissa."

George shook my hand and then they walked through the living room and out the front door. A moment later, light shone through the front window, vying with the rising sun.

Sarah stood and held out her hand to Sam. "Ready, Father?"

"In one moment. I wanted to apologize for who I became when I went into the smoke. For so long, I could not see clearly and I put so many people in danger."

"It wasn't your fault," Andy said. "The smoke makes you see things."

Sam shuddered. "I even thought I saw Carter pushing the lid onto the well. My guilt over not being able to keep the locket from taking him made me see things that weren't there. And, my sweet Sarah, burning..." his breath caught and he stopped. "But those things are no longer and I can see everything for what it is now and there is no reason for me to stay and watch over Culvers Grove." His eyes softened. "Not when it has you all to keep it safe." He tipped his hat and then turned to Sarah. "Can I have but one moment with Evie before I leave?"

Sarah nodded once and stood to the side. Sam and Evie went into the living room. Dad got up to get some coffee and Andy followed him into the kitchen, no doubt to raid the fridge.

"I'd better make sure he doesn't eat everything you own," Tristan said, following him.

"I could use something to munch on," Grant said, and nodded toward my grandma. "Give you a few minutes."

"Thanks," I mouthed.

Grandma took my hands in hers. "Marissa, you have become quite an asset to our line of seers. Don't ever let it go. Promise?"

My eyes filled with tears. "Do you have to go?"

She smiled. "Your grandfather is waiting for me. He'd be completely lost without me."

"I'm going to be lost without you," I said, hating the whine in my voice. "This is too much. Can't you stay for a little while?"

"I will come and visit you. I promise." She smiled softly. "When you smell bacon and biscuits cooking, know it's me looking in on you. I can't *wait* to see what you will become." She stood up and cleared her throat. "Now, I'm going to say goodbye to my son and I will see *you* later." She blinked rapidly a few times and then sniffed loudly. "I love you, Marissa, and I'm glad I got to know you."

"I love you, too," I said. I wrapped my arms around her and felt the energy pass between us. "Goodbye, Grandma."

She walked into the kitchen and I saw the doorway light up a few minutes later. I choked back a sob.

Sam came back into the dining room and nodded to Sarah. "It's time, my child."

Evie came up behind me.

"You okay?" I asked.

She nodded and grabbed my hand. "Bye, Sam. Sarah."

"Goodbye and thank you all for bringing us together."

They walked out through the front door hand in hand. Evie and I followed them out onto the porch, squinting against the rising sun and then shading our eyes with our hands as Sam and Sarah left.

The snow lay silent on the ground surrounding the farm. The voices of the boys and my dad laughing and talking in the kitchen were at our backs, contained within the walls that had somehow become my home over the last few months. I was infinitely grateful for the people who had helped me become who I was today and I would always be in their debt.

My friends had taught me that in this world, no one is truly alone.

I turned to Evie. "What did Sam say?"

She stared out at the snow. "He said that he will always hold a special place in his heart for me, but that I belong to this world. He wants me to live, love, and die a very old woman with gobs of grandchildren, who's done everything she ever wanted to do."

"And?"

She looked over at me. "That's exactly what I plan to do, St. Louis."

CHAPTER 33

"Try it again," I said. "It started to work."

Grant chuckled. "This is harder than Econ."

"Shut up and try again. You can get it!"

I watched the mirror in front of me for any sign of movement. My reflection sat cross-legged in the middle of my room on the carpet Evie and I had chosen in Chillicothe almost a year before. As I stared at the mirror, the middle of it began to ripple and pull away. In the distance, I could make out a figure.

"You've got it! Just a little more!"

Grant's face came into focus and he smiled. His dorm room was in the background and a tree of bright red leaves filled the window behind him.

"I can see you!" he said. "I forget how pretty you are."

I felt my cheeks rush with heat. "You were home last weekend and you'll be home again in a couple of weeks for Thanksgiving."

"Not soon enough. I have to go. We'll try again tomorrow night?"

I looked at the calendar on my phone. "Can't tomorrow night. We're going to a case in Tipton. A little girl keeps seeing a person standing at the end of her bed."

"Andy going?"

I nodded. "Yeah, I thought he could practice reading objects. See if he can find out about the person who lived in the house before."

"How's it going for him?"

I shrugged. "He and Tristan video chat every night, but it's been hard doing the long-distance thing. They'll be fine, though."

Grant smiled. "I meant, how's it going with his power?"

"Oh." I leaned back onto my hands, stretching my back. "It's taking a little bit for everyone to relearn using their powers."

"Was a lot easier getting them from you." He winked.

I smiled. "Well, Evie says it's like riding a bike."

"Well, tell Evie she had her bike a lot longer than we did."

"I'll text you tomorrow," I said. "Love you."

"Wish I could reach through and kiss you," he said.

"Training wheels first," I said. "Bye."

He waved and the image faded. My mirror returned to normal and I stood up.

Evie knocked on my door and stuck her head in. "Janice just drove up. Your dad says dinner's ready." She raised an eyebrow.

I sighed. This new cooking kick he was on was either going to make a world-class chef out of him or kill us all. I wasn't sure which would happen first. "What is it tonight?"

"Pad Thai."

At least it smelled good. "Maybe Thai is his milieu."

"How's Grant?"

"Frustrated that your powers came back quicker." I smiled and hung my jacket on the back of my closet door.

"Yeah, well, when you're good, you're good."

"You ready for tomorrow night?"

She nodded. "I had to cancel studying with Kaleb but I don't think he minded."

"Have you told him 'yes' yet?"

Evie shrugged. "Haven't decided."

"Would you quit stringing him along already? He asked you to the winter formal, like, a month ago!"

She smiled. "Come down soon. I don't want to be alone in there with the lovebirds."

"I'll be down in a minute," I said.

Evie closed the door and I heard her footsteps on the stairs. I stood staring at the photos hanging on my wall. Janice had been able to find photos of nearly our entire family tree in a box in a forgotten corner of the historical society. I smiled as I looked at the picture of my grandma. In the photo, she was a young girl, maybe seven. She had a short-cropped haircut and a large bow on the side of her head. She was wearing a white dress that I imagined it took sixteen people to wrangle her like a feral cat into. Her stockings had fallen down to reveal skinned knees and she held a stick horse in her hand, but looked like she would rather have thrown it at the cameraman than ridden it.

I ran a finger over the picture of Sam on a scaffold of the courthouse. Sarah's wedding photo. Henry and George holding hunting rifles. Above them all was the picture of my mother. The one that had been in my dad's room. In it, my mom and dad leaned in toward one another; their mouths open in laughter. If I closed my eyes and listened hard enough, I could almost hear it. I took a step back, looked at the wall, and smiled.

"My family," I whispered.

"Come on, St. Louis! Dinner!"

"Coming," I said, turning off the light and closing my door behind me. I skipped down the stairs into the kitchen. "Smells good, Dad. Hey, Janice."

"Hi, dear. I brought another article about Culvers Grove."

"Cool. I'll take a look at it after dinner." I reached up to grab a stack of plates from the cabinet.

Dad leaned back against the counter. He grabbed my arm and nodded toward Evie. I took a deep breath.

She stood shuffling through the mail on the kitchen table. She thumbed through the pile and stopped on a large white envelope. Her brow furrowed and she looked up at my dad.

"What's this?"

I smiled. "Open it."

She put her finger under the flap and ripped it open. She pulled a stack of papers out and looked at the front page, her eyes scanning quickly. Her shoulders went down as her hands dropped, the papers landing on the table. Turning to my dad, her eyes filled with tears.

"You're adopting me?"

Dad smiled. "If you'll have us. Genevieve, since we met you, you've been a part of this family."

Tears spilled out of her eyes onto her cheeks. She laughed. "Of course, I want to be part of this family!"

Dad took off his glasses and wiped his eyes with the back of his hand. I glanced over at Janice. She was full on crying, her plump cheeks red and wet.

"Do we, like, hug now or something?" Evie smiled through her tears.

"Yeah, sorry, it comes with being part of the fam." I held my arms wide. "We're huggers!"

She laughed and we stood in the kitchen hugging, the setting sun shining across the linoleum at our feet.

"Welcome home, Genevieve."

Yes, we were finally home.

Acknowledgements

Thank you to my husband and daughter. You are my everything. Always.

My sincerest appreciation goes to Christina Benedict, whose endless support helped craft this book from the first word. Thank you also to Michael and Amanda Booloodian for their ideas and suggestions when I was stuck. Thank you to my amazing readers, especially Josh Stone, who asked all the hard questions. Thank you to my various writing groups – without your support and humor, I would be lost. Thank you to my wonderful editor, Frankie Sutton, for her feedback and attention to detail; to Covered Creatively for another beautiful cover design, and to Vicki Deiter for her formatting expertise.

About The Author

Adria Waters is the author of the Ghost Hunters Society series and has seen ghosts all her life. She loves exploring the paranormal and goes on ghost tours in every place she visits. When she's not hunting ghosts, she loves torturing her family with road trips across the country to see every single sightseeing opportunity in the United States. Adria lives in Missouri with her very patient husband, her not-so-patient daughter, a herd of cats who insist that they are human, and various little spirits that pop up to say "hello" once in a while.

You can find out more about Adria and her writing at
www.AdriaWaters.com